# Friggin' Alice

# FRIGGIN' ALICE

a novel by **Bob Vokoun**

*For Glor*

# chapter 1

"FOR CRYIN' OUT LOUD, Richard!" Dad yelled as he slammed open my bedroom door and kicked my bed. "I told you last night that we were going. So get your lazy rear up outta that bed and get moving! Now!"

My bed shook again from a second quick kick to the mattress.

"Your mother expects me to spend more time with you boys so we make deeper connections," Dad said using air quotes. "So today, the three of us are goin' out to play a little golf. I want both of you dressed, fed and ready to go in thirty." His deep voice lingered in the air as he walked away.

Dad always barked his commands and knew that we would be totally compliant. Frank Strong always expected compliance; not just from his kids, but from everyone. Most of the time, people did what he asked, and not out of fear or a sense of obligation. People obeyed Frank simply because he acted like a leader. Or, maybe it was because they were told that he possessed a ridiculously high IQ. On more than one occasion, I heard him 'confess' to a friend that he was a genius. What a crock.

What he did possess was better than average looks tied to an athletic body; Dad stood 6-2, and weighed 210. He also took great pride in the ownership of a successful manufacturing company and even more when others sought his business opinions. I thought those were the top reasons he arrogantly believed he was superior to others. But contrary to my beliefs, Dad had many friends and they appreciated being around him. Whenever I overheard acquaintances talk about Frank, they respected him. And once they did, they ultimately did anything he asked. "I'm like magic," he'd say to us with his condescending smile.

At home, Dylan and I lived with the real Frank. He shunned outsiders and trusted no one. It seemed to us that he didn't give a rat's ass about anyone but himself. Frank truly was a man of many faces.

We had played golf with Dad on several other occasions. Like all the times before, our golf outing was something he wanted to do tied to what Mom asked. Even though we already knew this outing wouldn't be much fun, it was the only chance we ever got for a little father-sons time.

I dragged myself out of bed and shuffled down the hall to the doorway of Dylan's room. I looked in at the piles of his clothes and accumulated junk that covered every inch of the floor and wondered how anyone could find anything in this sty. I couldn't. But Dylan thrived with this type of disarray and never wanted to organize anything. Without warning, I banged the bedroom door against the wall and kicked his bed just like Dad did to me. Dylan mechanically sprang to a sitting position and pretended to be coherent. "What?" he moaned as he rubbed his eyes.

"Get your butt outta bed, D. We got thirty minutes to be in the car for golf with Dad, so... get up now!" I barked my instructions using my most adult voice. For most of this summer I heard a bass voice as it began to erupt from me, just like Dad's. It didn't happen all the time yet, but I wanted that voice to be mine.

Dylan whined, "Tell Dad I don't want to go. Tell Dad I'm too tired to play fetch for him. Then tell him that stupid big boy voice you're trying to use sucks the big one." Dylan stuffed his head under his pillow and lowered his voice an octave as he said, "Get out, I'm tryin' to get back to my last dream."

"Just get up, butt wipe. If you don't, you know what he'll do if you're not ready."

Dylan sat up again and stretched. "Fine, you win, I'll get up. Look, I'm up already." He stood up and took a swipe at me, and missed. "But today you're gonna be the one who's gonna fetch!" He grunted his disapproval with every movement as he put on his "golf" clothes.

I flung his door against the wall again for fun and headed back to my room as I practiced making my voice deeper, "Sometimes you act like such a girl."

If you don't already know, Dylan and I are twins. Most everyone believes that we are identical, but we're not. I am older by almost four minutes and I know that I'm much better looking. When Dad first stood over us in the crib, he called us two sides of the same coin. I guess most people could say that. Physically, we're the same size and weight with good bodies that'll eventually be like Dad's. And I've got to admit that our outward appearances are very similar. So we might be considered identical—if you're colorblind. The major reason we're not identical is because of our hair. Mine is brownish with red; D's is more red than brown.

When I say Dylan's hair is red, I'm not talking about a good red. It's that ugly orangey-red color that's usually found in depressed European countries. Dad has said that he and his two brothers all had different shades of red hair when they were born and by the time they were teens, the color was nearly identical. Good for them. Right now Dylan and Dad both have the same ugly Scottish yucky-red hair. "True Scotsman," Dad would bellow at him sometimes, in some weird dialect. Like in all history, there wasn't a Scot who had absolutely cool brownish red hair. Really!

When thirty minutes on the dot had elapsed, Dad yelled for his 'caddies' to "get their stinky buckets into the car this instant."

We hurried our butts into our seats. Truth be told, Dylan and I actually enjoyed being in his car. It was the only place where we got an opportunity for some alone time with Dad without his usual interruptions. Dad's car, a brand new Mercedes sedan, with plush leather interior and automatic everything, became our place to talk about anything. Or more accurately, Dad talked about the things he believed were important and that we should definitely know. These talks happened as he drove and were typically about how he saw the world. "You've got to learn the tough lessons if you want to excel in this world. There are people out there who will try to hurt you, and then there are those who will become your life-long friends. You need to understand who is who. Since the day you both were born, I've tried to show you boys how to become real men, to be Captains of Industry."

Yeah, Captains, good talk. Whatever.

As soon as we got to the first stoplight, Dad abruptly turned around in his seat, looked hard at both of us and said, "Are you two clean? You both better be clean. I mean it. And stay clean. The last time you two were in this car, you made a huge mess, remember? That's not going to happen today, is it?"

We sat silent. We didn't look up at him or even acknowledge that he had said something. Neither of us had accepted responsibility for spoiling his precious car. Neither of us showed the least bit of remorse either. We thought it wasn't such a big deal that we had tracked in a little bit of dirt our last time in his car, but according to him, we purposefully dragged in a ton of filth onto the back seat and all over the carpeting. This single heinous act of so-called disrespect caused life as we knew it to suddenly stop until the entire mess was cleaned. Dylan and I wasted an entire Saturday afternoon vacuuming and polishing the entire car to a showroom-new shine.

"Not today, right, boys?" he repeated more emphatically.

"Yessss, Dad," we replied in unison. Our attempt to irritate, like all others before it, was ignored. He knew we'd do as we were told.

We kept our mouths shut for the entire ride and I was slightly disappointed that our usual man-to-boys conversations didn't happen. Probably due to Dad's irrational fear of dirt getting into his car.

Once we arrived, I opened the door to get out and was blasted with the overpowering smell of fresh mown grass along with an intense buzzing sound that seemed to be all around us. Both irritated my senses.

Dad always called this 'his fairway as far as the eye could see'. But it really wasn't anything like that. Our 'course' was an open strip of private land owned by the electric company, located between two exceptionally tall electrical high tension towers. Each tower was connected to others with massive cables that carried electrical power to cities miles from here. The current that sped through the wires made loud buzzing noises that sounded like a swarm of angry bees that come chasing after you once their hive has been upended.

This became our golf course because Dad knew the guy who mowed the grass between the towers. Whenever he mowed, Dad got a call and we would go 'play golf'.

The space between the two imposing metal giants measured about 100 feet across so the only worry Dad had when he played here was to hit every ball perfectly straight. One hundred feet was a pretty narrow space to land every drive. An imperfect shot could carry into one of the homes that tightly abutted both outer edges of the electric alleyway. Dad told us that if he ever muffed a shot, we should hightail it as fast as we could to the car, get in and don't look back. It never happened. He was a great shot.

"Get my bag out of the trunk, Richie." That's what he called me, Richie. Not Rick like normal people but Richie, because he said that it sounded like money.

Today, I got lucky and caddied while Dylan retrieved, or, as we called it, 'fetch.' I hated to fetch. So much running and no conversation with Dad. Dylan hated it too. But I convinced him that he needed the extra work catching fly balls if he wanted to get onto the school's baseball team. He knew I was yanking his chain because he was already great in the outfield. D accepted the chore begrudgingly and told me that the next time we do this, no matter what, I had to go to the outfield and fetch. I agreed, but I knew I'd find a way to get him to do it again.

Dad popped the trunk and I hauled his clubs out to our tee box. There were way too many clubs in his bag which made it heavy and cumbersome. Even so, when I carried his clubs, he noticed that I tried to look like a real caddie. He liked that. "A good golfer should have a good caddie to help him with his game." Dad also believed that a good golfer should have every kind of tool in his bag. As he explained it, "The more weight in the bag, the better the golfer." What a pile.

"Tee the ball up, son," Dad said as he watched Dylan run down the 'fairway'. Dylan sprinted hard and continued to run until Dad hollered out a loud 'yo' and then he stopped. I teed the ball at exactly two fingers above the ground. Dad always said that two fingers was the exact ball to ground ratio the pros use. Two fingers would net the greatest drive distance without giving the ball the excessive lift that occurs when it's teed too high. "If you want to be a scratch golfer like me, son, these are the things you must know inside and out. Got it?" I heard his golf directives in my sleep. With every swing, he accurately launched ball after ball arrow-straight onto his fairway between the twin buzzing towers.

At the other end of the long drives was Dylan, prepared and wanting to make the best of today's activities. As a good Chicagoan and avid Cub fan, Dylan made sure that he wore his best Ernie Banks jersey. He also brought along his favorite baseball glove, a pro quality signed by Billy Alverez. Billy was a little known and quickly faded star that Dylan liked because when Billy played, he played with style. Dylan liked anyone who played with style. He stood in the field exactly where Dad had indicated with his shout. Each time the incoming drives were hit, Dylan caught them. After each catch, Dylan fired the ball back to me. I'd glove it and tee it up for the next shot. Dylan was excellent at fetching. He rarely missed.

Today, everything was going great and Dylan had zero misses. I could tell that his confidence level was sky high. I heard him as he talked to himself and pretended to be the game announcer with a crowd as they cheered him on after every play. "Another spectacular grab by the rookie phenom of the century, Dylan Strong." Then he'd make the crowd cheering sounds. For the entertainment of his imaginary adoring fans, he began to emulate his favorite old school outfielders. He'd make an over the shoulder running catch followed by a breadbasket grab a la Willie Mays or, to make things more of a challenge, he allowed the ball to get close to the ground which forced him to dive and catch it like Andre Dawson.

"Lookin' good, D," I yelled as he tossed the ball back.

"Tell me somethin' I don't know, Rick."

"Son, stop foolin' around and hand me the 4-iron," Dad directed. Dad disliked it when Dylan showed off and when I wasn't ready with his clubs. I reached into the bag and fumbled through the myriad 'special' clubs. "Come on, son, what takes you so damn long every single time?" I finally located the club and handed it to him.

"I want to show you something," Dad said without even looking my way. "Watch what I do. After I shoot, I'll expect to see you do it just like me, understand?" Dad stood over the ball and gazed down his fairway. Then, he declared, "I'm going to give the ball some draw, get it to move from right to left. Watch closely, son, you'll be doing this in a minute."

I stood behind him to get the best view of his swing and stance. I took everything he did into account. I watched how he stood, how he gripped the club and how his body turned as he struck the ball. I studied everything he did and it became everything that I wanted to reproduce. Just as he struck the ball I felt a gust of wind blow past us.

As if the ball were pre-programmed, it rocketed off his club and flew perfectly straight for nearly 200 yards. Then, just as he had said, the ball softly curved left. "See that! Now that is a thing of absolute beauty!" he roared, pleased with his golf prowess.

Dylan lurched to his right after the ball turned sharply and began its rapid descent away from him. His cleats dug in deep and he pushed himself to run as hard and fast as he could toward the plummeting object. It became obvious to me that Dylan had decided that he would not allow this drive, or any drive, the chance to hit the ground. He saw this catch as crucial, a matter of personal pride. Dylan quickly closed the gap between himself and the ball as he fully extended his gloved hand. He leaned forward as far as gravity would allow and readied himself. The ball was almost in his glove and he was about to complete the ultimate impossible catch when his foot snagged on something lodged in the grass. For a split second Dylan lost sight of the incoming projectile. As he straightened and looked up, the ball careened hard off his skull with a loud cracking noise that Dad and I heard all the way back to our makeshift tee box.

In that moment, time stood still. Dylan stopped in his tracks, grabbed the top of his head and deeply grimaced from the sharp pain. By the look he had on his face, I knew it had to hurt big time. As he attempted to take his next step forward, his glove fell off his hand and he dropped hard to his knees. I watched as his eyes closed and he fell face first to the ground.

"Holy shit!" I screamed as I bolted toward Dylan. My eyes were glued on him because I needed to see him move an arm, a leg, anything. But he didn't. My mind created grotesque visions of what I'd find when I got to him. Would he be dead? I saw vivid images of his crushed skull with blood that hemorrhaged everywhere. I cringed.

After I finally got to his side, which seemed like it took forever, Dylan appeared to be trying to sit up, but couldn't. He was still way out of it. So, I sat close, pulled him upright and held onto him. It wasn't long until his eyes fluttered and then suddenly blinked open large.

"How are you? Can you hear me?" I yelled into his face. I waited another minute until I felt he could understand what I was saying, then I said, "Man, you need a lot more practice in the outfield fetching!" I smiled. "Really, Dylan... are you OK?"

Dylan put his hand on a visibly growing knot atop his head and looked upward as if he could somehow see the lump as it grew. He made an 'ouch' face as he rubbed his lump but smiled at me as he said, "Betcha I still start in the outfield on the school team."

"Not after I tell everybody about this." I laughed.

Dylan was still holding his head when he pointed toward the car and grunted, "Where the heck is he going?"

I looked where Dylan motioned and saw Dad as he threw his clubs into the trunk of his car. He turned to us as he shut the lid and yelled with disgust, "Richard, when that brother of yours finally learns to stop showboating and just catch the damn ball, then the two of you two can come home."

Dylan and I sat on the grass and watched as Dad started the engine and drove off.

"Screw him," I said as I wrapped both of my arms around my brother. "It's you and me. No matter what, we'll always do everything together. Deal?"

"Deal," Dylan replied as we bumped fists.

# chapter **2**

DYLAN AND I HADN'T played golf with Dad for almost a year. He was always too busy or out of town. Whenever his booming voice summoned us, we were concerned. More often than not it was because he had decided we did something wrong. Or worse, when he thought one of us had to be punished. Dylan and I always made sure we sat in the exact same spots on the couch—so Dad knew which one was me and which was his problem child Dylan.

Dad called us to the living room in the middle of the day. We had no idea why he bellowed, it didn't matter—we were expected there immediately. I asked Dylan if he remembered doing anything to piss Dad off. He didn't say anything, he just shrugged and gave me one of those 'I don't know' looks.

As soon as we entered the room, we both stopped and stared as Dad shared a champagne toast with a woman we'd never seen before. Dylan and I watched in wonderment as they smiled at each other and sipped. It was definitely strange to see Dad so infatuated with this woman but, if you ask me, I didn't think she was anything special. I'd describe her this way—younger than Dad for sure, tallish with skinny legs, brown hair that curled at the shoulders, too much makeup and an obvious negative attitude toward twins. I saw it in her eyes right after Dylan and I came into the room. She didn't like us. Everyone knows instantly when someone doesn't like them.

"Boys, I want to introduce you to someone real special to me. Someone who has made me realize how exciting life could really be." Dad turned to this woman and raised his glass to her. "Boys, I want you to meet your new mom."

"Oh, please Frankie, let's not be so formal. They should call me by my name." Alice forced a smile in our general direction, then gave Dad a wet kiss. Yuck. Strings of spit hung out there as she pulled away. That was gross. Once she finally took the time to consider us again, she condescendingly quipped to Dad, "Now which one is which?" Then she let out this fake laugh as she added, "Oh, never mind, I'll learn their names soon enough."

All at once she stopped laughing, glared at us and looked sorta angry—but not. She acted like she could barely tolerate us and at the same time wanted us to know she ate puppies for breakfast or something. "Call me Alice. Alice Strong." She added a wink and held up her hand to show off her new large wedding ring. Her fingers wiggled as she broadly smiled and acted like the ring held magical powers. Without taking her eyes off her prize, she half demanded, "We're gonna be best of friends, aren't we boys?" Then that bitch actually reached out and tried to tweak my cheek.

"No thanks, we don't want a new mom," Dylan curtly replied which stopped her pinchy cuteness.

Dad took a step toward Dylan and used his 'I'm the Dad' voice when he said, "You don't get a vote here, son. Neither of you do." Dad faced Alice and smiled as if he had just solved all the world's problems.

He obviously hadn't and he couldn't be serious. This stranger should never be allowed in the same home our mom made for us. If Dad actually took a minute and asked for our opinion, we'd tell him that we didn't want or need her. Why would he?

Our mom had been the most incredible person in the world. She was kind to everyone and hardly ever yelled at us. Even when Dylan would make a mess, she would wrap us together in her arms and call us her 'joy boys'.

That was before Mom got real sick and had to go to the hospital. We weren't even allowed to go and visit. When Dad finally told us what happened he said it was pneumonia with complications and that she was suddenly gone. Even now I can't say that she died. Dad told us that the doctors did everything they could to save her, but that she was with the angels now. That was the only time I ever saw Dad cry. I did too, nonstop and I didn't care who saw me. Dylan locked himself in his room—I heard him sob through the wall.

I remember everything about the day of her funeral. I hated being there, but Dad told Dylan and me that we had to be like little soldiers for Mom. At first, when we got there, I saw her in the casket and it looked to me like she was asleep. She had on her nicest dress and laid there very still. I kept wishin' that she'd open her eyes, jump up and yell 'surprise'. We'd all laugh at her joke and get to go home. But once we got close enough and I touched her hand, it felt cold. I wanted to cry right then, but I wouldn't.

Throughout the service and reception afterwards, everyone said stuff to us that seemed unimportant. All sorts of people came up, held our hands or kissed us on the cheek and told us how awful they felt. Most of them we never had seen before. Dylan and I were surprised when we were introduced to a whole bunch of Mom's relatives that we didn't know we had. All of her side of the family attended and everyone was so upset. Grandpa Romano, Mom's dad, told me that Mom had been sick with pneumonia on the day she got married and he thought that was the reason she was so susceptible. When I asked what that meant, he told me to ask my father.

Even with people all around me I felt so alone that it hurt. Once the day ended, it became clear to me that I wouldn't ever be happy again, which made it impossible for me to believe that our dad would know-ingly open our door to some complete stranger. But there she was. Friggin' Alice.

Dad marched to his liquor cabinet and poured himself a drink. He spun the ice in his glass a few times and eventually came over and sat on the hassock in front of us. His expression softened as he stared into both of our faces and started over. "I know this must be a little bit of a shock. But before you jump to the wrong conclusion, I want all of us to go out for dinner so you both get to know Alice. She's nice, you'll see. We've got lots of things that we like to do together."

Dad took another sip of his drink and continued to ramble. "And, she likes kids... even though she never had any of her own. We've talked a lot about you boys and I knew from the start that we would all hit it off." Dad smiled at us as he stood and chugged the rest of his drink. There was an uncomfortable moment of silence and we knew that he expected us to say something. But from our viewpoint, he had already told us what to think and how we should feel.

"Well, men," Alice said as she picked up her purse and started to the door. "I'm off to unpack my things. And Frank..." Her voice was rigid as she directed Dad while she pointed at Dylan and me. "This would be a good time for that little conversation."

"Yeah, sure, Alice." Dad crossed the room after he blew her a kiss and settled into his easy chair. He shifted his weight from side to side as he uncomfortably tried to locate its soft spot. Eventually he repositioned himself on the front edge of the chair and said, "Isn't she great?" He paused, became sterner and finally blurted out, "I want you boys to like her."

Neither of us responded.

Dad looked at the ceiling and let out an exasperated sigh. He started over, this time he sounded less demanding and more sincere when he said, "Guys, your mom was the best person ever, but I need someone with me." He looked into our faces and saw blank looks. "Boys, do you understand what I mean when I say a man needs something more? Well... I miss the things adults do and Alice likes to do those things."

We still didn't respond.

Frustrated, Dad stood and scratched the back of his neck. He looked right through us—like he had more on his mind. Something was definitely wrong. He always scratched his neck like that when there was bad news. "And there's something else I gotta discuss with the both of you." Dad slowly walked over to the window and blankly stared outside. He acted like he didn't want to say what he had to say. Then he began, "We had a talk, I mean Alice and I had a talk, and we decided that both of you would be better off if you attended a school that builds young minds and bodies into strong young men." He sounded as if he were quoting some obscure pamphlet.

"So boys, here's what's we've decided... the two of you will be enrolled at the Garfield Military Academy.

It'll be fun. They're well known and have really cool programs." He finally turned and looked for our expressions. I'm sure they weren't good; I know mine wasn't. But Dad continued anyhow and even counted on his fingers for emphasis. "Hey, they'll teach you all about guns, you'll get boating lessons and best of all, you'll get the in-depth Martial Arts training you've always wanted!" He hoped for any sign of approval. As if those words could make their decision to pack us off to military school acceptable.

Dylan stood up, clearly upset. "So, let me get this straight, Dad. You decided to marry this strange Alice person without us even being there and now you've decided to ship us off to military school. Is that about right?"

"No, that's not exactly what I said. You've got to look at the bigger picture, Dylan. This is your golden opportunity to set your own standards, get a quality education and learn all kinds of really fabulous stuff." Dad eyed Dylan and waited to see his reaction.

"Bullshit!" Dylan screamed into Dad's face as he ran out of the room. Once he got to his bedroom, he slammed his door and yelled louder, "You are so full of bullshit!"

After Dylan's tirade, Dad turned an impatient eye towards me. His words were cold now when he said, "Listen, Richie, this is for your own good. So stop your bitching cuz you've got no idea how much money this'll cost me. Well I'll tell ya... it's a damn pretty penny. So if you think an argument will work this time, you're sadly mistaken. Alice and I decided that we need time alone to enjoy our new life together and you boys need discipline. Two birds. One stone. Case closed."

"Then I want to go live with Grandpa Romano. He wouldn't…"

"No!" Dad cut me off. "You and your brother will do as I say. Understand this—it's time to become men. In one month you and Dylan will be starting military school." He then added, "For Christ sake Richie, stop acting like such a baby. You're getting older now, it's time to start acting like it." He went to his bottle, poured another drink and walked out of the room without saying another word.

Life as we knew it had suddenly changed.

# chapter 3

AS SOON AS ALICE was unpacked, she took control of everything and decided that we were no longer welcome in our own house. She instantly turned Dad against us and purposefully made our lives difficult as our remaining days at home quickly passed. When that day arrived, Dad forced us to pack all our junk into a suitcase and put them in the trunk. We sat quietly in the back seat as he drove us to the academy. For the entire trip, we had no conversation. Dad didn't even turn on the car radio to listen to tunes, not even the news.

Once we got to the academy, Dylan and I were unceremoniously dumped at the front gate. Dad just popped the trunk lid and told us to unload our own luggage. We stood with our bags in hand and watched as Dad and Alice drove off. Neither of them even bothered to wave goodbye. I sat on my suitcase and stared at the car as it disappeared from my view. As it passed the first ridge, the car's radio came on and music wafted back down the hill.

I looked around and noticed two sneering gargoyles perched on opposite sides of the old rusted gate entrance of Garfield Military Academy. They annoyed me. I thought this must be what prison looks like.

Neither Dylan nor I wanted to go past the gate and onto the grounds. We sat on our luggage and considered the possibility of running away. Unfortunately, Dad made that idea impossible because, between the two of us, we couldn't rub two dimes together. I jokingly suggested to Dylan that he should consider selling his body to science so we would have enough money to start the trip.

Dylan flipped me off and launched into some colorful language when we were greeted by a kid who said he was responsible for our orientation. His name was Thomas Rubin. He had a friendly face with a wonderful broad smile. He wasn't very big but when he spoke, he stood tall and obviously took pride in what he did. Impressive kid, we liked him.

Thomas pointed the way as we picked up our suitcases, cautiously walked past the sneering gargoyles and started toward our new home. Thomas understood our situation and that we didn't want to be there, so to loosen us up he started by talking about himself. He said that he was the youngest son of a prominent Miami judge and that one day he was going to follow in his Dad's footsteps. He spoke and carried himself with such confidence that even though I had just met him, I knew he'd do it.

He mentioned that he'd been at the academy for almost a year and was excited to attend. The more he rambled, the better Dylan and I felt. Because of Thomas, we started to think that this place wouldn't be so bad after all. He became our bright spot in an otherwise crappy day.

After Thomas got his personal bio information out, he paused, cleared his throat and started into his prepared school speech. "OK guys, listen up," he inhaled deeply and began. "Welcome to Garfield Military Academy. As your official guide I'm here to conduct your personal orientation to the Academy." He stopped and clumsily used a sweeping hand gesture that started at the gate and finished as he motioned to the school buildings. "You may not know this, but the GMA was originally developed by a great wartime hero, General Martin Garfield, with the assistance of huge individual private donations. Everything on the campus from the buildings to the curriculum was designed to his rigid specifications. Many students here at GMA are the children of the rich and famous. Which could be a good thing or a bad thing—I personally think mostly bad, but I'm not supposed to say that. The academy provides every young man an excellent education and, if you bust your ass, you'd receive the same kind of training that you'd get at a full-blown special forces training facility. Yeah, it's a unique place," he said a bit too amped up. Thomas took a breath and throttled back on his enthusiasm. "Want to hear more?" he asked.

"Yeah, sure, kid. Knock yourself out," replied an uninterested Dylan.

Without missing a beat and ignoring Dylan's attitude, Thomas continued. "Located on a sprawling 100-acre estate, the GMA's five large buildings have been completely redesigned to replicate the architectural style of civil war Georgia."

"I got more, wanna hear it?" Thomas said.

I nodded.

"All five buildings hug the shoreline like a horseshoe around the southernmost edge of Lake Historic. The main building is for dining and housing. The students call it The Square cuz of its square shape. Unbelievable, right?" Thomas grinned. "That is the building where everyone eats, sleeps and studies. Four staircases are located on each side of the building for our convenience. The other four buildings are classrooms and lecture halls, plus we have the sports facility, stables, and the boat dock." Thomas concluded. "You'll know about everything soon, any questions?"

For the balance of the day, we hung out together and he showed us around campus. Dylan and I liked Thomas. Over time, we became great friends. From our point of view, Thomas was like the little brother we never had. We stayed close, and to us, he was family. Thomas would always say, "In order to survive in this place we must have close friends."

Dylan and I knew Thomas was right and we realized early on that we couldn't let our guard down. For all we knew, we might be stuck here forever. That was a depressing thought. "Look at it this way, D," I said, "We can get smarter, get stronger and before you know it, we run this place."

"Yeah, sure we will, Rick," Dylan scoffed. "How about we just go with the flow and learn as we go."

# chapter 4

DYLAN AND I WORKED diligently, kept our noses to the grindstone and made major strides forward to improve our grades and our physical selves. Interestingly enough, we also noticed how much more similar our appearance had become.

Since we arrived, very few people could tell which one of us was Dylan or which was me. We were often misidentified. Most people actually thought there was only one of us. One day, for our personal entertainment, we exchanged places in all our classes. We fooled every one of our teachers and every student except Thomas. The charade was fun. I personally thought it would be a no-brainer to figure out who was who. I obviously have the better personality.

For our physical entertainment, we spent crazy amounts of time doing sports. Individually, or as teammates, we became proficient at so many things. But the discipline that Dylan and I really enjoyed and spent ninety percent of our free time doing was Martial Arts. We worked out for hours every day and our efforts were rewarded with black belts. Any time we were paired as teammates, we were unbeatable—even when we fought against older boys.

One of the more troublesome older boys that we quickly learned to stay away from was a kid named Marco Winston. He was large, creepy and overly enjoyed his position as the school bully. Marco only picked on defenseless kids and seemed obsessed with younger boys. He demanded that they do as he said, when he said.

To call people out, Marco sat in his third floor dorm window with one leg inside the building, and one leg outside with his butt on the sill. His dorm room perch overlooked the main path to the other buildings and became his personal throne. Every day he sat there and yelled out to kids as they passed. He always wanted something from them and demanded that they immediately come up the stairs to his room and bring it to him. The kids he picked on were always small and had rich families. They feared his retaliation, so they would march up the stairs and pay his tribute. The word around school was that Marco would sexually abuse the littlest kids. We instantly disliked him.

Because we really didn't want or need any more trouble, Dylan and I went out of our way to avoid Marco. Unfortunately, we knew that it was only a matter of time until he did something or we didn't do something that would ignite the fuse.

Late one afternoon, after we finished a grueling workout, Marco snuck up behind me at the water fountain and tried to give me a wedgie. Dylan saw him as he came at me and shoved him aside before he could do any damage. Marco bounced off of a nearby wall and banged his head. A small cut opened over his eye and it started to bleed. As soon as Marco checked his wound and saw the blood, he angrily lurched at us.

"Stand down, cadet," roared Captain Lang who stood just behind Marco at the fountain. "Or feel what it's like to be one of my test dummies." Captain Lang was the Martial Arts instructor who regularly used disobedient students to illustrate painful wrist locks or debilitating holds in his classes.

"He pushed me!" complained Marco.

Captain Lang stepped close to Marco and yelled in his face, "One week! Would you like another, cadet?"

"No, sir," replied Marco as he glared at Dylan and me.

"Then get the hell out of my face," the Captain demanded. His intense glare stayed on Marco until he walked off.

Captain Lang then focused his ire on us and said, "Both of you cadets, get back to your rooms immediately." The anger in his voice startled us to attention. We immediately turned and marched where we were told.

But the damage was done. The embarrassment Marco sustained had already spread across the entire academy. Students began to talk about how we kicked his ass and made him bleed. Marco couldn't allow himself to be humiliated. We knew that it wouldn't be long until he tried something desperate to get even.

Later that same evening, while we were in the main dining hall, Marco snuck up behind me, reached over my shoulder and stole the apple off my plate. I turned and watched him as he flipped it back and forth from one hand to the other. Then he spoke as if he were talking to everyone in the hall as he said, "What's yours is now mine. Everything you've got is now mine."

Marco had to do something to regain his lost stature. He acted supremely confident because he saw himself as too big for me, or anyone, to handle alone. Marco was a load, for sure. I was big for my age, but still he was bigger.

"Give it back," I demanded of Marco, as I got up from my chair and positioned myself for the inevitable fight. I slowly and calmly stated, "I'm only going to tell you that once."

Dylan stood and took up my right flank. I set my feet, clenched my fists and readied myself for the first punch. Several of the nearby students moved back and away from the table as they sensed the upcoming confrontation. The room got quiet as Marco took his first step toward me.

"Stand down this minute!" The booming voice of the academy commandant, Commander Mitchell, shot across the hall. He stood and watched to see if any one of us was stupid enough to disobey his direct order. "That is unless you cadets want permanent kitchen duty. Maybe a lifetime with pots and pans would cool you off."

This wasn't the time for a fight, but still on the ready, Dylan and I waited for Marco to stand down. We watched him closely and expected that he would try something even after the rebuff from Commander Mitchell. Marco took a bite of my apple, dropped the rest of it to the floor and spat the bite out at me. He threw on a nasty smile as he loudly stated for everyone to hear, "Later, girls."

I looked over at Dylan as he muttered, "What a dill weed, Rick. We're going to have to deal with that ape someday soon. Let's make sure we do it together, just for fun, OK?"

"Sure," I smiled. "That does sound like fun."

Later that night, our friend Thomas Rubin was severally beaten and according to the rumor mill, also raped. No one had to say who had done it; we all knew. Thomas was beaten so badly that he couldn't even speak. His eyes were swollen shut, he had a deeply split lip and a compound fracture of his arm. We all knew that Thomas was a message sent to me and Dylan. The poor kid didn't stand a chance in a fight like that. Thomas was taken by ambulance to the local hospital. Unable to speak and identify his attacker, the Academy said they would wait until Thomas could talk before they would start an investigation.

I saw the look of rage and disgust on Dylan's face when we first heard the news.

I shook my head and said, "That son of a bitch must pay for Thomas. You in?"

"I'm in," Dylan said with zero hesitation.

# chapter 5

OVER THE NEXT TWO days, Dylan and I developed our plan. We spied on Marco and noted his movements as he went to and from classes. Our plan had to be simple and had to look like we were never involved. We ran over the details until we were sure that it would work. By taking Marco down, we wanted to send a message to everyone at the school. That message was that Marco's time was over and that this type of animal behavior wouldn't be allowed.

The two of us went to bed early that night, but neither of us slept. This was the first time in our lives that we would purposefully try to physically hurt someone.

We rose early, ate breakfast, and went outside, hanging out in front of Marco's room. We didn't want to look too obvious, so one of us would leave while the other would hang. Eventually, Marco came to his balcony and comfortably sat on his windowsill throne.

"Hey, you, Strong," he yelled down, as he finally took notice of me. Marco wanted to create a spectacle for everyone to see. "I want some money now! If you know what's good for you you'll get your ass up here now."He laughed to himself with the belief that he was totally invincible.

I looked for Dylan, our eyes met for a second and our plan went into action. Dylan turned and went to the side of the building. He climbed the east staircase that wasn't typically used by many students at this time of day. I kept Marco's attention and verbally played with him.

"Easy, big boy, don't strain your little brain." I wanted to make sure Dylan had ample time to get all the way upstairs and to Marco's door unseen.

I looked around at the faces of our friends who stood near me. In each of them I saw that they wanted to help, but couldn't risk their involvement. I mouthed "Don't worry", but I could see that they didn't believe me.

"Twenty bucks. Bring it now or I'll come for you later."

I sighed and played the part as I entered the stairwell directly in front of me and slowly climbed the stairs to Marco's room. His door was open. I easily heard him as he yelled down at other students, his voice echoing down the hall.

By the time I reached the right side of Marco's door, Dylan already stood on the left. I felt waves of nervousness pass through me. I checked out Dylan and saw that he wasn't nervous at all. He stood and nodded at me with a 'let's do this' grin on his face.

Dylan obviously wanted this guy more than I did. As I replayed the plan in my head, I felt a rush of concern not knowing exactly what to expect. If this didn't go right, it could turn ugly. Marco was big and fast.

I knocked one hard fist on the door.

"It's open, you idiot," Marco bellowed.

I heard him as he continued to yell to boys down below. "Hey, you little plebe, I'm coming to visit you tonight."

Marco's comment made my blood boil. This jerk actually believed that no one could ever stop him. I entered the room and walked quickly to the far side so that if Marco looked, he wouldn't have seen Dylan as he entered behind me and moved to the left.

I looked at Dylan as Marco repeated his threat out the window to the young boy below. That was it and we wouldn't take any more from him. Dylan and I rushed Marco, grabbed him by his pant leg and quickly tossed him over the sill and out of the window. We backed up into the room so onlookers wouldn't see us. To anyone below, it would look like Marco lost his balance and accidentally fell.

From inside Marco's room, Dylan and I heard Marco scream like a little girl as he plummeted. That sound was followed by a thud which resembled the sound of a watermelon dropped onto concrete. Immediately after his fall, and to our surprise, the students below his window erupted into a spontaneous chorus of loud cheers. Dylan and I exchanged satisfied grins.

Dylan quickly exited Marco's room and made a beeline for the staircase. I took my time and came down the stairs just as a growing crowd encircled the crying and broken Marco. An ambulance arrived soon afterward.

The injury that Marco sustained left him with a permanent limp. His parents were outraged and pulled him out of the academy. The school obviously was too violent and wasn't the right fit for their son.

An inquiry into the accident was immediately taken up by the academy board of directors. They were obligated to determine if there was foul play involved. They were also deluged with calls from parents who insisted on a fast resolution to this problem. Since I was Marco's last quarry, the board of directors automatically assumed that I was to blame. Even though the entire student body stood behind us and proclaimed our innocence, the academy was forced to cover their collective rear ends and appease the school's wealthy contributors. The decision was simple—expel both Dylan and me.

Early the next morning, the two of us were escorted to the academy gates and told to stand just outside the school property. We quietly stood and listened to Commander Mitchell. He sounded relieved and disgusted at the same time as he said, "The Academy has investigated this situation thoroughly. After exhaustive examination, we can't conclusively prove that you two were responsible for this terrible event. But I know damn well you did it."

The Commander reached out and put his hand on one of the rusty gate halves and slowly pulled it closed in front of Dylan. "As a matter of fact, neither of you has contributed one iota to this school. You've disrespected our time-honored traditions and have purposefully been nothing more than a pain in my ass." He moved to the second half of the rusty gate and pulled it closed in front of me. As he aligned the gate halves, he looked down on us through the bars. "The board and I have unanimously decided that you two are no longer welcome. Good day, gentlemen."

Commander Mitchell let out a disgusted grunt as he closed the creaky gate latch in front of us. He turned his back and slowly ambled to the academy without us.

chapter **6**

"YOU LITTLE DOGS, I don't care which one of you took it, just give it back to me!" Alice screamed after she found her jewelry box empty. "Your father gave me that necklace for my wedding gift, now give it back!"

Seated together in our usual places on the front room couch, Dylan smiled and I snickered. Another plan successfully accomplished. Over the last few months we had planned the details of various schemes which we now precisely executed, one at a time. Our sole objective was to piss Alice off.

Since we got bounced from the military school, the two of us had become a pair of thorns in her side. And we'd just started. We knew she was the one who convinced Dad that it was somehow in our best interest to be kicked out of our own home. When we confronted her with those obvious facts, she denied ever being a part of that decision. She unscrupulously blamed Dad for everything. We knew better. She was such a liar.

"Duh, what are you talking about, Alice? What you lookin' for? We didn't do anything. Dad must have taken it."

Red faced, Alice reached out and grabbed both of us and squeezed as hard as she could. Her entire body shook with anger. "Keep screwing with me, you little bastards, and you'll be sorry. One day, very soon, I'll show you who's the boss."

As she grew angrier, Alice began to unintentionally spit her words at us as she continued her rant. "Your father is going to hear about this. I'll let him handle the two of you. The next time..." Alice suddenly stopped her tongue-lashing, stood and looked away from us. Her hands trembled as she said, "I'm done with the two of you."

This was a win. Every time we pushed her buttons so that she got angry, we won; even if Dad punished us. Our punishment for this type of stunt was never the same. A lot rode on how Dad felt when he got home from work. If he had a good day, we might get off with a stern warning. A bad day, on the other hand, could net us serious problems.

It wasn't long until we heard the garage door open and Dad's car pull in. Alice met him at the door as soon as he entered. We listened to their conversation through the walls. It was mostly Alice's voice going on about something missing and that she can't control us. What we didn't hear was Dad's voice, which always meant that we were in deep trouble.

Dad walked straight into Dylan's room and sat on the edge of his bed. We tried to read him to see if it was a good or bad day. He didn't move, he just sat there and swirled his drink. Dylan and I moved deeper into the room and waited for him to explode.

After he slowly exhaled, Dad looked at us and said, "Really, boys?" That was the only comment he had after he was forced to listen to Alice's long explicative-laced rant. "I didn't even get a sip of my martini before she lit into me about one of you stealing her diamonds." He took a long sip, swallowed and said to the two of us, "Just give them back."

For the first time in our lives, he gave us an opportunity to make it better. Unfortunately, I didn't stop myself and wisecracked, "Don't got it, I think she musta lost it and is trying to get another one from you."

Rage instantly flashed across Dad's eyes. In that moment I knew I'd gone too far. I was afraid he'd decide to beat us like he had when we were expelled. The beating and subsequent grounding was the worst punishment he'd ever given us. Even worse than being sent away. He had made it clear that he wouldn't allow any disrespect of him or Alice. He especially went ballistic when we compared Alice to Mom.

Dad stood and paced back and forth in front of Dylan's bed as he angrily stated, "How many times do we need to have this conversation boys? Your attitude toward Alice is unacceptable—Change. It. Now! I'm sick and tired of playing referee." Dad looked exasperated. "The next time you guys do something like this... I'll be forced to put you both to work. The choice is simple—realize how good you have it or pay for the privilege of living in MY house."

Without a thought of consequence and before anything could be done to stop him, Dylan yelled back, "Alice will never be our mom."

That was the moment when our summer vacation vanished and two boys got kicked out of their home again.

"Boys, meet Ed Johnson," Dad coldly stated as they both looked down at us. "Ed is your summer boss. You're going to be staying here with him while the two of you paint his entire house inside and out. You will do what Ed says. Understand?"

We stood quietly as we looked at our new boss man, Ed. He didn't seem so special. He was one of Dad's clients and more than willing to use us as slave labor. He was about Dad's age, a bit shorter and sorta fat. He sported a disfigured leg that obviously caused him a great deal of pain.

"I don't want any trouble from you boys, hear me?" Ed dictated, to show our dad that he was in charge. "There's plenty of work to be done."

Dad scowled as he looked at Dylan and me. "I had better not get a call from Mr. Johnson about you two. I'm counting on you boys." He said nothing more as he turned and left.

"This way," Ed directed. He took the lead as he walked us around to the back of house. We couldn't help but notice Ed's red swollen knee and the look of pain on his face every time he stepped. As we stared, Ed said, "I got the gout, boys. Feels like gravel stuck in my knee joint. Hurts like hell." Ed led us to the front of his garage, pointed at the door and said, "This will be your summer home... 'til you get my place painted. That's the deal. So... try to make yourselves comfortable."

Ed's garage was old and looked more like a run-down shed in need of emergency repair. Dylan swung open the creaky side door and a half dozen spiders scurried out. The place reeked with the smell of old people and motor oil. We peered into the space and saw two ancient army cots which were set up in the center of the room. They were barely visible because so little sunlight came through the garage's only window. The window was covered with dirt and one of the four panes was broken. There was also a lawn mower and an assortment of yard tools piled in the corner. The floor around the edges of the garage was littered with leaves and dirt.

"Home sweet home," I said as I plopped on the first cot. A cloud of dust floated up around me. "Friggin' Alice."

Dylan sat on the cot next to mine. He made a yuck face and reiterated our mutual feelings. "Friggin' Alice."

From outside our garage room, Ed bellowed, "Breakfast is at seven, boys, lunch is at noon and dinner is at six. If you ain't clean and ready, you don't eat. Got it?" Ed acted like a drill sergeant who was told that we were going to be a problem. "Tomorrow morning we start bright and early."

At seven sharp, Dylan knocked on the back door of the house. "Come on in." said a female voice inside the house. We guessed it was Mrs. Ed.

"Hope you two are hungry. Oh, by the by, I'm Naomi," she said as she smiled and held out her hand to shake. She shook both of our hands and held them just long enough to make us feel uneasy. Naomi was much younger than Ed and had a youthful appearance. She knew she was pretty and that she had a figure teen boys dreamt about. Whenever we looked her way, we caught her staring at us. It was strange but she was sorta cute and all.

After breakfast, we went outside and Dylan joked, "She wants me."

I thought about it for a second and said in return, "She's yours."

Once we got into our job, we realized that painting was hard work. This job had begun to look like the punishment that would never end. Days turned into weeks of outside work in the summer heat. We scraped, primed and painted every inch of the exterior of Ed's house. It was drudgery and tiring. By the time we'd finished a day's work and eaten our dinner, we barely had the energy to drag our butts back to our cots and pass out from exhaustion. We were glad that Ed put an alarm clock in the garage or we would have easily slept through breakfast most every day.

Fortunately for us, all bad things must end someday and our work on the exterior mercifully concluded.

The only thing left was Ed's evaluation and approval. It was obvious from the minute he started that he wasn't going to give either easily. He took his time and strolled around the entire house as he scrutinized every bit of our work. His hands stayed on his hips while he closely peered at, examined and reexamined every exterior detail. When he felt fully satisfied with what we had accomplished he said, "Good job on the outside, boys. Yeah, real nice. Couldn't have done better myself." He turned and limped toward the rear of the house as he said, "I got more for you to do around this way." As he entered the back door, Dylan and I followed closely behind. We watched Ed's painful stride that seemed different today.

Once inside, he pointed and said, "I want you boys to start painting here in the living room. After you've put two coats on the ceiling and the walls, then you'll move upstairs. Two coats, hear me? The paint and brushes are in each room already. Don't screw this up," Ed seemed unusually brusque as he ordered us to work. His face was redder, more pained than normal. "I'm gonna have to see the doctor this morning. I'll be gone for no more than three hours. By the time I get back, I expect to see those two coats of paint on the living room walls. Get to it, boys."

Ed left without fanfare as Dylan and I got to work. After we moved furniture, spread out the tarps and taped all the woodwork, we were ready to get painting. We started on the ceiling, put up two coats and went on to the walls. Once the first coat was up on the living room walls, we realized that the color they chose had to be a mistake. It was a disgusting baby-poopish ugly grey. After we finished, we stepped back and looked at what we'd accomplished. The color looked so bad that it reminded me of something I flushed that morning. We were positive there was some sort of color snafu. No one with any taste would intentionally put this much ugly into their home.

"We should stop and not put up the second coat," I told Dylan. "We should wait 'til Ed gets back."

"Yeah, but you heard Mr. Ed. He wants it done."

We debated whether or not we should apply the second coat until we heard Mrs. Ed as she moved around upstairs. Dylan shrugged his shoulders and lifted his palms while he raised his eyebrows. My interpretation of that move was, "should we call up and get her to decide?" I silently nodded approval to Dylan's idea. He walked to the staircase, looked at the top landing and yelled up to her, "Hey, Mrs. Johnson, can you come down for a minute? We need your help with something. This color you guys chose doesn't look right."

Dylan looked my way and gave me the same shoulder eyebrow thing. I gave it back. We waited but didn't get a response. "Mrs. J, no one else is here to decide, so please come down. This room looks like a big mistake." Dylan attempted to coax her down.

We soon heard footsteps moving toward the staircase. As the sound of her footfalls came closer, Dylan and I moved to meet her. Once she came into view, we both stopped and stared in total disbelief. My mouth must have been wide open because Dylan reached over and pushed it closed. But right there, to our absolute amazement, was Naomi as she came down the stairs with nothing on, except a towel that she wrapped around her wet hair, and red high heeled shoes. Other than that, she was—oh, my God—totally naked.

This was crazy unbelievable. Our wildest dreams had just come true in Mr. Ed's living room.

Dylan and I openly gawked at Naomi as she continued her angel-like descent. She coyly smiled as she lightly ran her hands over her hips and provocatively asked, "What do you think boys? You like?"

We couldn't move, we couldn't talk, we were frozen like the kids Naomi knew we were. Compared to any magazine woman, Naomi was totally more beautiful. She had something special that was so hot. I didn't want to, but I knew that I swallowed hard as she moved past.

I checked out Dylan. He was standing like a human statue. His eyes were fixed on every move Naomi made as she floated around us. He even sounded really tense as he blurted out, "Yeah sure, you're hot. Not the best I've seen." He clumsily repositioned himself and assumed his coolest stance. He hoped she'd notice. She didn't.

Naomi already knew she was hot and that Dylan had never seen anyone like her. We stood transfixed as she slowly but purposefully sauntered around the living room and gave us a view that demanded our continuous unbroken attention. When Naomi eventually looked my way I was sure that I was trembling. She cozied up so close in front of me and started to get real playful as she used both hands to pull on the collar of my shirt. She was giggling a little as she pulled me closer. I felt the warmth of her naked body against me. She was so beautiful. All I could do was stare into her blue eyes. I was totally hers.

"WHAT IN HOLY HELL ARE YOU TWO LITTLE BASTARDS DOING TO MY WIFE?" Ed screamed.

We had no idea he had returned home. We stood motionless. We didn't know what to do.

"I'm gone for ONE DAMN MINUTE only to find you two degenerates MOLESTING MY INNO-CENT WIFE..." he shrieked even louder.

Then I saw him pick up a hammer and charge toward me. His face was bright red and his eyes were bulging out of their sockets as he yelled even louder, GET OUT! GET THE HELL OUT OF MY HOUSE NOW!"

Ed charged at us and repeatedly swung the clawed weapon. Dylan and I quickly angled past him and barely avoided injury as we rushed to the back door. We swung it open, ready to escape, but we couldn't leave, not yet. Not when our sweet naked Naomi had already started to provocatively ascend the stairs. We stood half-way out the door and reverently watched her every movement until she looked back over her shoul-der and slyly winked. Naomi had given us the gift of a lifetime. But alas, far sooner than we wanted, she was gone. For our sakes, we hoped that she would confess and tell Ed that this entire incident was her fault. But she didn't.

The back screen door slammed closed. As we walked away, we listened to Mr. Ed through the open window as he sorrowfully moaned to his wife, "Aw Naomi, not again."

We started down the dirt road—Dylan and me truckin' home after we got kicked out of yet another place. We expected Dad would go animal on us when we got home. Been there, felt that.

# chapter 7

THE WARMTH OF SUMMER beckoned as our senior year of high school mercifully came to an end. Between pranking teachers and avoiding detention, school was exhausting. In the fall we would be off to college to embrace our new adventures, or so we'd been told. Until then, we had a plan—to fritter away as much time as we could doing as little as possible.

Our goal seemed so simple. We wanted to devote ourselves to the pleasures of doing nothing—which any recent graduate would openly admit was an honorable undertaking. We dreamt of the allure of blissful relaxation. We seriously believed that this summer, unlike every other summer, would include fun. Unfortunately, on the day we graduated, we were reminded that Dad's roof was still under the supreme rule of Alice. In her wicked kingdom, fun did not exist. To emphasize her resolve toward us, Alice convinced Dad that this summer we needed to experience something that would keep us busy and well out of her sight. This year Dad and Alice arranged a special kind of hell for us. I'm sure they saw it as full-time employment without a chance of leniency.

The Rightway Can Company made tin cans. RCC made tin cans the way they were made in the early 1900's. They started with the raw materials which were printed, cut and soldered using antique machinery and techniques that seemed incredibly time and labor intensive. The obvious inefficiencies caused by their adoption of antiquated production processes must have deeply cut into profits. To eliminate expense, RCC ownership located their factory in one of the oldest and cheapest buildings they could find in the warehouse district.

The RCC factory was a three story monstrosity erected in 1902 that spanned an entire city block. Each floor was designated for a specific segment of the can making process. The first floor was for shipping, both truck and rail, and for storage of the company's entire supply of tin. Tin storage filled three massive rooms with row after row of twenty foot tall stacks of metal. Each stack consisted of hundreds of individual sheets of tin—milled to various thicknesses and quality grades. The second floor was for finishing and packaging. Workers in this department stood at the end of long conveyor lines and packaged the newly created cans for shipment. The top floor was where the large produc-tion equipment was located. Eight massive machines that individually weighed tons created thousands of cans daily. Ear-deafening metal-on-metal noises along with the smell of hot solder filled the air on the third floor as the machines shaped the cans into their final forms. When the factory was running at full capacity, a constant line of trucks and train box cars were filled with product all day, every day.

With three shifts in full production, RCC employed over five hundred workers. Every man and woman employed there worked hard and received excellent union wages for their efforts. This gig was dirty and strenuous, but the money was better than anything Dylan or I could get on our own.

"Welcome to Rightway," Sims Pitman said in an overly officious voice as soon as we walked out of the men's locker room wearing our dull grey work clothes. Sims was a bald bird-like man in his early thirties who got his position at the company because his father, our current HR manager, Ralph Pitman, had pulled some strings. Sims was determined to show his daddy how important he could be to the company. We guessed it was why he acted the way he did as he curtly demanded, "Follow me down to the tin plate department."

The tin plate department was responsible for cutting large tin sheets into smaller specific widths for the creation of tin can lids and bottoms. Slitters, as the machines were called, had circulating scissor-like blades at the end of a long metal tabletop. Using an edge guide, the operator would carefully slide every sheet through the blades of the slitter. Once the tin was slit, the strips were collected and stacked on a nearby skid. Each man in the department was required to push two tons of tin through the slitters daily. Everyone in the department was accustomed to the strenuous back-breaking work. I couldn't help but notice that all the men were bowed from a lifetime of bending, lifting and stacking excessive weight.

If the work wasn't difficult enough, the working conditions in the department were deplorable. The machines, floors and walls were encrusted with what looked like generations of accumulated filth that compacted black into every corner. The only daylight that did stream into the department came from small windows placed high on the outer walls. The sun's rays reflected a fine silt that constantly hung in the air and made me feel like I couldn't get enough to breathe. It was obvious that this place was not built for the well-being of its workers.

Sims handed us paperwork and dumped us at the office door of the tin plate department without any introduction to the department manager, Anthony Marretti. We walked into his office, introduced our-selves and put out our hands out for him to shake. He glared at our friendly gesture and harshly erupted, "Did I invite you college twerps into my office?" He waited half a beat for an answer as he snarled even louder, "Then get the hell out!"

"Yes, sir." We quickly exited.

From all outward appearances, Anthony was the type of guy who was born with a chip on his shoulder. He stood only 5ft 4ish, but was powerfully built and definitely looked tough enough to make sure no one ever screwed with him. We quickly realized that he hated almost anyone who thought they were better than him—especially college boys. He didn't like college morons at all. Why should he even try to be nice to the people who would eventually look down their overly educated noses at him. So today, as we stood in front of him, he wanted to make it perfectly clear that he was the boss. We knew right then that the most demeaning jobs imaginable would be reserved for his stupid college twins. What could I say, boss man Anthony was a real sweetheart.

Day after day, our work was always physically strenuous and mentally numbing but we came to see that the people we worked with made it bearable. We found some good people with good hearts. We also identified some bad people, some psychopathic, even a few despots. It didn't take us long to differentiate friend from foe. Mutual misery sometimes made odd bedfellows.

Amid all the personality types in our little microcosm was one guy who stood out above everyone. He was an extremely charismatic man named Gatlin Brown or Gat, as he preferred. Gat possessed that special something which made everyone around him feel comfortable and relaxed. I don't know what it was exactly, but he owned an inner confidence which when tied to his outward strength made him magnetic. Both Dylan and I were drawn to him and saw him as a natural born leader.

Even though Gat may have been all that to us, he constantly demanded privacy and refused to be in the spotlight. He made it a point to keep a low profile even to the extent of wearing camouflage clothing every day. He quipped that camo made him invisible, especially to the bosses. Day after day he'd drive his forklift truck throughout the building as he picked up loads of metal from one machine and delivered them to other points in the RCC assembly process. As he made his pick-ups and deliveries, he would engage in conversations with his many friends. We found out later that once Gat considered you his friend, you became part of his family circle. Gat's circle was formidable with a vast network that kept him informed about everything that happened in the neighborhood and throughout the company. Even the Hillbilly militants who claimed that they weren't afraid of anyone or anything stayed clear of entanglements with Gat and his people. Just in case. An uneasy truce was struck between the two, but like a powder keg, it was ready to blow at any minute.

One hot day, boss man Anthony felt particularly sadistic and sent Dylan and I to the train shed to clean out box cars. Word was that the box cars were usually disgustingly hot and littered with dried feed corn that needed to be swept out. We were also informed that the box cars were full of rats that got caught inside the cars as they fed on the corn. So the scare was, after the rats spent several days in the hot locked box cars they were dying of thirst and had been known to attack anyone as they scurried out.

Neither of us were overly excited about the prospect of thirst-crazed rabid rats gnawing on us. So, I decided that if there were rats, one of us should sacrifice himself for the other. Dylan refused.

To make this event even more exciting, boss man Anthony made sure things got even worse when he saddled us with our 'supervisor of the day,' Billy Walenski. Billy was big, stupid and acted arrogant for absolutely no reason. Word on the street was that he had recently failed the State Trooper's exam for the fifth time and now couldn't be the cop he'd always dreamt he would become. Billy outwardly fumed about this as he walked ahead and mumbled under his breath the entire way to the train shed.

The shed itself was nothing more than a tall wooden structure big enough to hold five or six train cars in a row. The train tracks ran through the center of the building. Dual raised loading platforms flanked either side of the tracks, which facilitated easy loading and unloading. Open ended to accommodate the box cars' easy entry and exit, the inside space was designed specifically to keep the train cars away from the elements.

Once I got close, I was surprised to see that the train cars were much bigger than I expected. Each car had two huge heavy sliding doors, one on either side, that were connected to the cars. Sets of large rusty rollers ran in tracks under the doors on the side of each car. Today, we had three cars lined up and waiting to be cleaned. All we needed to do was slide open the door and walk right in. Can't wait.

"You boys know whatcha supposta do?" asked Billy as he readied himself for the doors to be opened. "There's probably a couple rats in there. So when the door opens, you best get the hell out the way cuz... they gonna bite ya." He glared at us bug-eyed and made an exaggerated ratlike expression with his front teeth.

Dylan was not amused as he threw open the latch on the first car. Together, he and I grabbed onto the door handles and pulled hard as we strained to slide open the box car door. As the door slowly gave way, loud screeching noises erupted from the rusted rollers as they scraped and dragged along their filth-caked track. From inside the car, the shrieks of dehydrated rats overwhelmed all other sound as they simultaneously rushed to escape captivity. The narrow space that we'd opened instantly filled and was insufficient to accommodate the number of vermin as they frantically attempted to exit the boiling hot train car. Dylan and I quickly grabbed onto the door handles and jumped up onto the door as it slowly slid open. Frenzied rats ran from inside the car and madly scurried in every direction just below our feet.

Before we could turn around, Billy pulled a small revolver out from under his shirt and began to blast off round after round at the fast-moving rodents. We clung to the door as it slowly opened and feared his bad marksmanship plus the real possibility that one of us may be catching a stray bullet. As the vermin scurried away, the idiot cop-wannabe kept shooting until he ran out of ammunition. Billy stood on the dock and cackled like a demented zombie, "You boys lucky I didn't clip ya."

"What the hell!" Dylan yelled as he jumped down from the door and got into Billy's face. "You think that's funny? Then, tell me if this is funny, Gomer." An angry Dylan jumped and threw a flying side kick that landed hard under Billy's chin. As Billy flew backwards, I noticed that his feet had to be a good six inches above the ground. He bounced once as he hit the concrete of the loading dock, out cold.

"Do you believe that asshole?" I asked a satisfied Dylan. "And I'll bet we're gonna be the ones who catch some shit for this."

"Who cares, let 'em try to do something."

We walked slowly back to the tin plate department and left Billy lying on the concrete snoring. We expected that there would be some sort of instant backlash from his people, if he had people. We'd been at the can plant long enough to know that people always had to have friends.

Within an hour after we returned to tin plate, Gat rolled up on his forklift and said, "I hear you two been causin' a little ruckus in the train shed and kicked some white boy ass this afternoon. Got to tell you, this kinda news travels fast around here. I've even heard some talk of retaliation. Seems you got some nasty types real unhappy and a few flat nose degenerates decided that you both should meet an untimely demise in the parking lot about five this afternoon. Just thought you boys might be interested." Without waiting for our response, Gat rolled off to attend to his other disciples.

"Shit, Dylan, whether we win or lose, Dad isn't going to like this."

Dylan rolled his eyes and started laughing at me. "Really, Rick? You and I are going up against the Hillbilly Nation after work and you're worried about what the old man might do? Hell," he laughed even harder now, "you probably won't even survive the fight."

"Kiss my ass!"

"Brother, you may be extremely good looking, but you're not my type," he said still laughing.

The workday ended and Dylan and I walked outside into the parking lot ready to kick the stuffing out of anyone that stood up to us. This wasn't the first time we fought together against bad odds. Not surprisingly, about a dozen or so beefy grunts were there to greet us.

"Hello, morons," Dylan started. "Which one of you inbred bitches wants a little of what I gave to that dipshit Billy?"

With that comment, the melee began. A few of the younger men who felt lucky stepped in first. We took care of them quickly. Now emboldened by numbers, seven or eight guys gang-rushed us. Dylan and I fought back the human onslaught as we kicked and punched anyone who came within our reach. Together, we held our ground and did some damage of our own. Dylan taunted his opponents and told them where he planned to hit them just before he did. Blood flew everywhere. I knew for certain that we dropped six or seven of these guys. But as soon as one would go down hard, another guy would step in ready to fight against us.

Somehow in all the madness, I missed a block and caught a hard right that sent me backwards and down. In an instant, three guys jumped on top of me and held me down, while others threw punches and kicks that landed hard all over my body. I looked up and caught sight of Dylan out of the corner of my eye. He was still pounding away, but I could tell he was beginning to tire. Just then, I was hit across the face with a club or a nightstick and my world started to spin. For the first time in my life, I felt like I was going to black out.

I flailed my arms at unseen opponents as I desperately tried to refocus. But everyone and everything around me was blurred. From out of nowhere, I felt someone grab under my arm and lift me back to my feet. I held onto that arm long enough to steady myself and when I looked back I saw the guy who just rescued me. It was Gat. He and some of his circle of friends joined our battle and came to our side just as we needed them. I clawed my way back into the fight and with the help of Gat's circle, we saw their numbers quickly diminish. Dylan, who was now feeling that victory was within our reach, actually smiled after he knocked out another opponent. He stopped fighting, walked straight up to Gat and bear hugged our friend. He literally lifted the man off the ground and held him there. We knew the bad guys were on the run.

But this was the most dangerous time of the fight. Because the conclusion isn't final and dirty tricks with evil intent come to the surface. Through all the mayhem, I spied a tall man holding a knife as he moved fast toward Gat's back. "Dylan," I screamed, "behind you!"

Dylan moved swiftly as he spun between Gat and the tall man. He threw a front snap kick that shattered the man's hand. I clearly heard a loud crack followed by his painful howl. Dylan finished him off with a hard right that knocked him to the ground.

A relieved Gat turned to Dylan as the one-handed man crumbled at their feet. He knew Dylan had protected him from harm—may have even saved his life. The two men embraced as Gat promised, "At any time, for any reason, if either of you need me... I'll be there."

"We love you too, man," replied Dylan for both of us. "But the real of it is—you're the one who saved our asses today, Gat."

Dylan looked my way and we locked eyes. He had a look of true satisfaction on his face along with his patented smile. Then he turned to the crew who had saved our butts and said, "Who's ready to go grab some beers? Rick's buyin'!"

# chapter 8

COLLEGE ENDED LONG BEFORE we had enough fun and Dylan and I were forced to face the reality of joining the real world. For as long as I could remember, Dad boasted to anyone who would listen that both of his boys would work for him after we graduated to help grow his company. He repeatedly drummed into us that this was our legacy and we should be grateful. We considered the legacy thing, dismissed it and focused on what it would be like to actually work for him. Right from the start we understood that our clashing personalities made it difficult, to say the least. But after we evaluated our situation, reality became clear—we needed to earn a living and the prospects of obtaining employment outside the company weren't bright. So, without any real consideration of other job possibilities, we both decided it was most expeditious for us to join Dad's company. Really, how bad could it be? After all, this was the plan since we were kids.

"Hello, Mr. Campbell, I think you want to talk to my brother, Dylan. He's our new VP of Sales. He knows everything there is about automotive brake parts. I'm his brother Rick Strong, the new VP of marketing here at FAS Inc." I lightly tapped on the desk to get the attention of Mary, my indispensable executive assistant. "Get me Dylan." I softly whispered while I held my hand over the receiver. "We've got a new client on the line."

Since Dylan and I came to work here, Mary had been my go-to person at FAS Inc. Mary was the one who showed us what to do and how to do it. She was the cog in the machine that made this company move, the keeper of all the secrets and instinctively knew how to apply just the right amount of pressure to get things done. She also had the ability to remember every client by name, along with the names of their spouses and kids. Believe me when I say, normal people can't do all she does and we were a far better company because of her.

Mary McCarthy was a single mom in her late 20s, smart, motivated and tough. She only took this job after her acting career in Hollywood was permanently put on hold. Her story was all too familiar. Mary was an aspiring actress and was noticed by some bigwig who told her she would become a star. She then fell head over heels for a kind man, who wasn't an actor, married him for a short time but eventually had to let him go. As she put it... "it didn't stick." I heard that he moved to Alaska or somewhere remote to do something with fisheries. But what the fish fanatic didn't realize was that he got Mary pregnant which, in turn, made the Hollywood bigwig disappear along with her budding acting career.

On the plus side, Mary had the most beautiful boy ever conceived. While Dylan and I lounged at the university, she attended night school and raised her young son while she worked full-time. She received her Bachelor's degree and graduated with honors. I couldn't help but be impressed. She's a special person.

Today, as I tapped on my desk, Mary simply politely mouthed the words, "Put him on hold and go find Dylan yourself." She turned away with a smile.

I put Mr. Campbell on hold and pleaded, "C'mon Mary... do a guy a solid."

"He's in the break room, smoking undoubtedly. He knows that he shouldn't do that here," Mary said as she held her nose. She hated the habit and often tried to get Dylan to quit. "I'll make you a deal," Mary continued with a coy smile. "If you're real nice to me and let me take the afternoon off, I'll get Smokey Joe for you."

I hesitated, but relented. "Sure Mary, It's a deal. Please get Dylan."

She gave me a slight wink as she turned to the lunchroom. "Thanks boss, you're my favorite."

Dylan sauntered into my office and broadly smiled. He knew he had landed another account. His ego grew as I watched an extremely confident Dylan launch into his sales schtick. "Hey Pat, how's it goin'? You missed the best part of the party, it got totally out of control." Pat laughed out loud as he responded. Dylan winked at me as he opened his computer. Competitive much?

Dylan had a way with people. He always did. Men and women alike immediately gravitated to him. I think if he asked anyone for anything, they would probably line up to give it to him. Unbelievable, but true. I don't have that kind of power over people. My power, if that's a real thing, is that I see the whole picture. Ideas come to me like images in my head. I take random concepts, piece them together and create successful solutions. I believe the biggest reason the business has grown since we've started is due to my clear thinking. I develop the plans and Dylan makes them happen. We are an unbeatable team. We really are two sides of the same coin, just like Dad always said.

Our working process started back at the academy and really came together when we were in college. We had an advantage as twins. So we exploited that... often. On some projects we joined forces and the two of us would work together toward a common goal or we made it appear that the same person was in two places at the same time. Hell, most everyone we knew thought we were just one person. It was easier to fool almost everyone after we aged and our hair color became identical.

What we eventually took away from college and applied to business was the realization that people don't pay close enough attention to the details that surround them. As soon as we started with the company, we employed our twins advantage and applied ourselves. We performed beyond Dad's expectations and the company's annual growth rate mirrored our efforts and rewarded FAS Inc. with a healthy corporate bank account.

We poured profits back into the business and expanded our internal capabilities which made us a sought after company. The interest in the company wasn't only because of our efficient production and manufacturing capabilities, it was because we attracted quality employees. With our insistence, the company did its part to keep quality people. We made sure every associate had health care coverage and a share of the profits. Our motto was that a happy workplace created a stable workforce that was unstoppable.

Unfortunately for us there was always one person in the company who didn't necessarily think this new style of business was all good news. What he saw was us hiring more employees and increasing payroll. When expansion was required, he only saw more loans and bills. This growth got someone very upset and that someone was Dad.

He openly expressed his displeasure to everyone in the entire company. One day Dad barged into the office and shook a crumpled copy of our latest profit and loss statement. "This isn't a charity operation. I don't care how big we grow or how many damn cars are in that parking lot. The only reason we are doing this... is to make money. Got it?"

Regardless of all the conversations that we had with Dad that clearly illustrated how we've improved the company, he refused to accept our processes. He never took the time to grasp what Dylan and I had put into place. Not only that, he couldn't or wouldn't accept that every person had to be treated with respect. This was a problem. Along with the fact that Dad still believed that the company wouldn't survive without his constant and unnecessary influence.

"I want us to sit down and discuss this in private, Richie, Dylan, Now!," Dad demanded as he stormed into my office, papers in hand. "We've got to go over our numbers!"

After a long week, both Dylan and I were exhausted and we were not in the mood for an argument. Moreover I was done with his micro-management and criticisms. I readied myself for a fight.

Dylan and I sat and waited for his latest rebuff. "All right boys, we're all together, what can I do for you?" Dad glared at Dylan, then back at me as he waited for our answer. He asked again, "Why did you call me into the office?"

When I looked at Dylan his surprised expression was what I felt 'what the hell'. I didn't want to over-react so I calmly stated, "You came in here just one minute ago for one of your little business talks. Don't you remember?" I waited a beat and restarted, "Dad... we don't have time for games today."

Dylan walked over to Dad and put his hand on his shoulder. "You do remember, don't you, Dad?" His question was gentle, not in his usual wise-ass tone.

Dad focused on Dylan. We watched as his expression changed from confident to unsure. It appeared he suddenly realized what had happened and he searched for a way out. "Sure, never mind, it's not important." He momentarily refocused and said, "Yeah, one of those business talks..." He looked down at his watch and blurted, "Whoa! I'm late, I've missed something that I should've..." He stood tall, straightened his clothes and without another word briskly walked out of the building.

"He's losing it," Dylan said.

"It worries me too D."

# chapter 9

"HERE'S TO ANOTHER YEAR of double digit growth," I happily reported. I lifted my champagne flute and toasted everyone in the room as our annual company party got underway. "The added effort that all of you put in this year has made us better. Better at price, better at quality and damn better at speed. Because of all of you, we are a better company. And to show our appreciation, we've written every employee a better bonus check!"

A loud cheer of appreciation rippled through the room. In mid-cheer, Dylan grabbed the mic out of my hand and let out a primal scream. The entire room full of people fell instantly silent and watched Dylan as he shouted, "Let's PAR-TAY!"

The band struck its first chord at full volume and the room went wild. All around us our friends, who were so instrumental in our success, enjoyed the moment. I watched as everyone young and old alike spun and danced to the beat. It appeared to me that we were all without a care in the world.

There were reasons for these festivities and I've got to brag. Our little company FAS Inc., short for Frank And Sons, (in reality it stood for Frank A. Strong) surpassed its best year yet again. By a lot. Most of our growth was due to our market program which I designed to directly link to sales. But I've got to admit, this year Dylan was the embodiment of the Midas touch when it came to sales. It seemed that with every call he made, the sales followed. I admitted to Dylan that the reason for our latest growth spurt was because of him. Yes, I actually said that.

The extra money that came with the growth allowed us to purchase equipment and expand our operations by adding a full second shift. More money and an expanded workload made our employees secure and happy. Dylan and I got happy too. We allowed ourselves a bonus and banked some real cash for the first time in our careers.

We both agreed that we should do a little more for Mary and reward her loyalty and hard work with a large raise, and because we realized how much we depended on her, we wrote her an additional personal check from the two of us for her to sock away for her son's college fund.

I instantly knew that Dylan and I did the right thing the minute Mary opened the envelope. I almost fell backwards at her reaction. She ran to me, wrapped her arms around my neck and hugged me hard as crocodile tears ran down her face. "You're the best." Then she kissed me on the cheek. For a feeling like this, I'd happily give up anything. She grabbed hold of Dylan and hugged him too. I was surprised to see Dylan tear up. It felt good to see him this way. This had become an all-around feel-good evening.

As the good times rolled on, Frank marched onto the dance floor. Without concern or remorse, he shook his fist at me and screamed over the music, "How much did you throw away on these people this time, Richie? How much did this cost me?"

"Dad," I stated firmly but respectfully in an attempt to keep his intrusion from becoming a scene. "Let's take this into the other room. We don't want to ruin this party!" I motioned to the band to resume and without waiting for an answer, Dylan and I led Dad into my office.

I shut the door behind him, showed him the seat in front of my desk and did my best not to explode. "Are you trying to screw up this celebration? I'm not sure what's going on here, Dad, but I'd like to know. You've been acting very strange."

Dad only stared in my direction. He appeared disoriented as he searched for the right thing to say. Or maybe his reticence was because he just realized he'd acted like an ass. Once he finally spoke, he sounded concerned or even a bit worried as he said, "I've got a lot on my mind. Let's just say that I need both of you boys with me right now."

Dylan stood over Dad and bluntly asked, "Is there something that you should be telling us? Are you sick or what?"

Dad looked up and locked eyes with Dylan. His fearful expression told us that something was wrong. Dad stammered, but for whatever reason, he refused to let it come out.

"Say it already. All this cloak and dagger shit only pisses us off." Dylan stated as he walked over to my liquor cabinet.

Dylan picked up the bottle of scotch, poured out three servings at exactly two fingers each and handed one to each of us. Dad sat motionless for a long time. Eventually, he got out of his chair and went to the window where he stood staring outside at nothing. He barely sipped the contents of his glass when he finally said, "I keep forgetting things."

He stepped away from the window, took a large swig of his scotch and calmly spoke. "It started years ago. I'd forget things. At first I wasn't concerned because it was just little things, like lost keys, forgotten appointments, things like that. Now, after what the doc just let me know..." Dad paused as he moved around to the front edge of my desk and found a place to sit, "I can't keep this to myself any longer."

"What's going on, Dad?" I asked.

His eyes were closed and I could tell that he was trying hard to remember something. Then, he blurted, "I'm losing my fucking mind."

"Whoa, Dad, we all forget things. It's not that bad," Dylan said.

"Son, I've still got some lucid moments, but my memory's so bad that I can't recall much from yesterday. I knew that at some point I discussed all this with Alice. Had to be at least two or more years ago. She made sure that I got examined right away by a neurologist. The diagnosis wasn't good boys. The doc told me that I've got early onset dementia, you know, Alzheimer's disease. Boys, I won't ever get any better."

"What the hell, Dad? Why didn't you say something? We could have been there and helped you through it all," Dylan said.

For no reason, Dad suddenly became angry. He stared at me as he pointed out the window to the parking lot as he spouted, "Your mother! She demanded we sell the house. She has been such a pain in the ass ever since the twins were born. And frankly, I don't want to deal with that right now."

I shook my head in disbelief. "Dad, what are you talking about? Does Alice want to sell the house?" I lightly probed.

He turned and angrily glared at me, "What did you say, Richie? Can't you see that I'm tryin' to tell you what that fucking doctor told me? Do ya think you could just shut the hell up and listen for a change?"

I shot a look at Dylan, then back to Dad as I calmly replied, "Sorry, Dad, please go ahead."

Still upset, Dad ranted, "He told me that my heart's screwed up. It's unbalanced or some such nonsense. Then, that arrogant little prick doctor actually handed me a damn pamphlet for some sort of hospice care bullshit. Said I should be lookin' into this right away. Dammit anyhow, this can't be happening to me. Not to me. I can't be losin' it."

Dylan spoke first, "Your heart? Dad, that's not good. You've got to slow down. Maybe this is a good time for you to step away from the business."

"No," Dad snapped back. "I still run the show until I can't. Remember, I made this company... don't ever forget that."

I reached out and put my hand on Dad's arm. I could feel his coiled tension as I gently said, "We're here for you, Dad, you know that. But first things first, we've got to think about your health and find ways to reduce the stress in your life. Dad, I know you don't want to hear this but, I think maybe it's time for you to retire. We've got this. And realistically... you haven't been in charge here for years."

Dad sighed heavily as he slumped forward, put his head in his hands and started to cry. I never thought my words could have hurt him so much.

"I'm your dad. I thought at least one of you would want to help." With tears running down his cheeks, he rose and marched out of the office. I chased after him and pled, "Dad, please don't leave. Talk to us!" The sounds of the celebration drown out my words.

Dylan fell uncommonly quiet. He refused to let me see how much Dad's news had affected him. Instead, he deflected. "I personally think it's that bitch, Alice. She must have done something that got him sick. Ever since she wormed her way into his life...." Dylan snarled.

We sat in silence, each of us lost in his own thoughts until the trill of my cell phone filled the room. I checked the readout, exhaled deeply, looked at Dylan and asked the caller, "Are you all right, Dad?"

"Richie, I need your help," Dad's voice sounded different... worried. "Please help me."

I've never heard Dad sound like things were out of his control. He was always in control. "What's wrong? Has something happened? Was there an accident?" I quickly asked without waiting for any answer. I put the call on speaker. "Tell me what's happened. Where are you?"

"I don't know, I can't tell where..." his voice sounded strange. He began again and attempted to reconstruct what went wrong. "I was mad at you when I left the office. After I got goin', I musta turned the wrong way. I... I can't remember. I don't recognize this neighborhood. I thought I was headed home." Now, sounding more fearful, Dad implored, "Richie... I think I'm lost. You gotta come and get me. Please, Richie. Don't leave me here."

"Just a minute, Dad, hold on." I turned to Dylan and whispered, "He's lost and he sounds really scared."

Dylan stood and shook his head, "Most of the time, our whole life even, that guy was a total ass to us. But......... he's still our dad."

I nodded at Dylan as I gently directed, "Get the car. Let's go get him."

# chapter 10

THE TEMPERATURE WAS IN the mid-nineties and the humidity neared unbearable as Frank and Alice deplaned in Orlando for their annual winter vacation. They stood in a long cab line full of airline passengers who had flown to Florida for a taste of the sun. Frank's impatience was obvious.

The two of them were there to visit Lew Vain, Alice's brother, and Lew's wife, Marge. Lew and Marge's home had become their winter destination every year for over a decade. And every year Frank expected to be treated like royalty because Lew's law firm handled the legal needs for FAS, Inc. Frank was positive that Lew had excessively billed for his services so from Frank's point of view, the trip was already paid for in advance. Frank's visit always brought discord to Lew's home.

"What's taking so long?" Frank blurted out loudly enough to get the attention of everyone stuck in the cab line. "You'd think your lazy brother would have the common courtesy to pick us up." Frank complained as he wiped the sweat off his face with an already soaked hankie.

Annoyed and embarrassed, Alice quieted Frank, "He's busy, Frank. Anyhow, you're tired and cranky. You know how you get when you're tired. No one enjoys your company when you're that way. Let's just take a quiet cab ride to Lew's and when we get there you can take a little nap. Sound good?" Alice questioned and directed at the same time.

Frank reluctantly agreed as he slowly edged forward in line, hot and uncomfortable. He shook his head just to see the sweat as it flew from his brow.

Before their guests arrived, Lew attempted to defuse the lingering animosity that Marge carried toward Frank. After years of the visits, Lew fully understood why she loathed being around Frank. It was Marge's home and from her perspective Frank was not welcome. She hated the idea of putting up with another visit.

"Can't you just tell them to stay at a hotel?", begged Marge. "Alice is barely bearable, but every year Frank does something that pisses me off. He thinks he's funny, but... he just screws with us."

"You're right, hon, ab-so-lute-ly. And this year could be the last year he ever visits. Just think about how nice that would be if what Alice told me actually comes true." Lew made smooching noises into Marge's ear as he squeezed her waist and tried to garner her approval. He could tell she needed more encouragement. He further confided, "Alice told me that Frank is losing it. I mean, she said all his short term memory is going away fast. Sad for him, huh?" he smirked and continued, "This is our golden opportunity to get some payback for all those years that we've put up with him. Soooo... Alice and I've got a little something brewing that should help compensate us for Frank's constant bullshit. She and I have decided that it is time to make a little financial adjustment."

"What are you talking about, Lew?" Marge asked.

Lew heard footsteps on the front porch. "Let's talk later. I'll lay out the whole plan for ya." He turned from Marge, put on a fake smile and opened the front door.

As soon as the door opened, Frank bumped past Alice and strode directly toward Lew. Frank reached out and quickly shook Lew's hand while he turned his head in the direction of Marge. He made a sour face and blew her an imaginary kiss. Then, as Alice had directed, he excused himself to take a nap. "I need to rest. I'm just a little tired. All this travel musta worn me out." Frank yawned in Lew's face as he slowly shuffled down the hall toward his bedroom, suitcase in hand. No one cared enough to say anything to him.

"He does seem different, Alice. He looks ten years older," said Lew in a low voice. "You weren't kidding when you said he'd aged."

Before she responded, Alice took a peek around the corner and watched Frank as he disappeared into the bedroom and shut the door. She turned back to

Lew and said quietly, "I've done all the prep work. He's totally convinced it's all for the good of the kids. I'd like to see where you are with the paperwork."

Lew wasn't prepared to jump right into business. Nevertheless, he nodded as he led Alice and Marge into his study and pointed to the overstuffed faux leather chairs in front of his desk. "Relax here while I find the folder." Lew plopped into his desk chair and rummaged through his file drawer. He located a thin file folder and handed it to Alice. "As far as I can tell, everything you asked for is in there."

Alice had a look of anticipation when she took the folder. She opened it and read its contents in less than a minute. She immediately became enraged as she threw the folder at Lew. "What the hell is this? Are you purposefully trying to screw this whole thing up? Everything was supposed to be ready for signatures this week, without fail. You do understand what 'without fail' means, doncha Lew?"

Peeved that Alice had berated him in front of Marge, Lew retorted. "This 'little manipulation' only started because you called me and asked for it. I didn't call you... remember? I'm the lawyer, you're not. So, in simple words that even you might understand Alice, if we do this thing incorrectly, we go to prison. And yes, I know what 'without fail' means."

Lew expected her to recognize his expertise and apologize to him. When it became obvious Alice would do neither, Lew eventually continued, "All right... I found a Florida law that'll do everything you wanted. I twisted the intent of the law some... but I'm sure it'll work. The only snag was that Frank has to be found mentally incompetent. To prove that he had lost his marbles, I needed a legal document written and filed by a state certified psychologist that clearly states Frank's condition. Fortunately, my law firm employs one of those guys. I had him develop a document that exaggerated Frank's mental health problems so that he looks totally unbalanced. It verifies Frank is incapable of handling any legal matters due to Alzheimer's. As his spouse, you are given power of attorney, health, everything." Lew stopped and stared at Alice. He waited for her approval, he even tapped his foot. Still nothing. He continued a bit more snidely, "After that, Alice, we've only got three things that need to be completed. My notary's required sign-off, his affixed seal on the document, and a hopeful short wait for Frank to die."

"Fine. But remember Lew, Frank may not be himself anymore, but he's not an idiot. If he ever gets wind of this...," warned Alice.

"Trust me, sis. It will be signed, sealed and delivered before the week is out and Frank will be none the wiser."

Marge interrupted. "Is this the thing you mentioned to me earlier, Lew?"

He nodded.

"Ooooh, tell me about it. You said you'd fill me in," implored Marge.

Lew shot a quick look at his sister to garner her approval to include Marge in their plot. Alice nodded back. He began, "This conversation can't ever be repeated, understand? No one can ever hear anything about what I'm about to say, not ever." Lew sternly looked at Marge. "One screwup, one comment to the wrong person and I'm not kidding, we're all in jail."

"All right, I won't say a word. Just tell me," Marge demanded.

"All right then." Lew sat back and started, "A couple years ago, Alice noticed that Frank began to forget things. She thought it might be a good idea to take a quick peek at his will—you know, to see what she'd get. She had no idea cuz Frank made sure his will was kept a secret. He'd often teased her and said that he had left her nothing. We thought that wasn't a nice thing to say. So, I checked out his will when they were here on vacation last year—he never knew, of course. Turns out Frank wasn't lying. He'd left most of his estate including the entire business to his boys and very little to Alice."

Lew paused and waited. He wanted Marge to see Frank as a cruel man who intentionally left Alice nothing. Lew felt Alice was owed. Lew pressed on, "You can see why Alice was pissed. All those years that she coddled him, took care of his unruly kids and fulfilled all his manly needs—hell, Alice should definitely get more."

"I had no idea." Marge nodded as she waited for more details.

"So I looked into this for Alice and unearthed an archaic law which was originally designed to aid couples when one of them becomes mentally incompetent after serving in a World War. In those days, legal documents were only written in the name of the man and if he was mentally addled, the family suffered. So a law was enacted and it contained a legal provision that gave spouses a legitimate process to alter documents when those 'special circumstances' were evident. Now, I know that the law wasn't specifically written for our particular purpose—not even close."

Lew paused. "But, I'm sure that if our position was challenged in court, we would simply state that incompetent is still incompetent regardless of the individual type of disability. We'd easily win. In the eyes of the law, what we did was legal and it gave us the right to amend Frank's will to read whatever Alice wanted it to read without him ever knowing. When Frank croaks, Alice gets a payday and so will we," Lew finished.

"Are you sure? It all seems a bit underhanded," Marge questioned.

"Well... any new version of a will can always be challenged in the courts. So if this one is challenged, I'm ready. My law firm has created a maze of documentation that would require an exceptionally good attorney, a boatload of money and a very large staff to eventually unravel. By the time the Strong boys figure out that they were scammed, the money, the business and everything of value will be long gone. The trick to our ploy is keeping it secret. If they can somehow prove that we conspired to alter the will for our own benefit, we all go to jail," Lew flatly stated.

"So they cannot and will not find out, period," an impatient Alice interjected. "Now that we're all up to speed, can you pull-eeze tell me when the documents will be ready for my signature?"

"Tomorrow," Lew chirped.

Annoyed that this ordeal hadn't concluded, Alice opened the sliding glass door and announced, "I'm out for some sun. Call me for lunch."

Marge acknowledged Alice's demand with a nod as Lew watched and waited for the door to close behind her. As soon as Lew was sure she was out of ear shot, he slid his chair close to Marge and privately continued, "Just between you and me... Alice demanded that she gets everything. She wants the house, the business, all of their savings, everything. She made a huge point of telling me that Rick and Dylan get nothing."

"Isn't that a bit harsh?" Marge asked. Then with an uneasy smile, she warned, "You'd better be careful, Lew. Alice is mean enough to bury us with the twins."

"I agree." Lew took a peek over his shoulder and made sure Alice couldn't hear him as he further confided in Marge, "For our benefit, I've put together a contingency plan—in case things get a little squirrelly and she decides not to give us what we deserve."

Marge repositioned her chair to watch the door for Alice if she returned. "Tell me."

Lew leaned into Marge. "Remember a client of the firm called Wanton Bank? They've been with the firm for a few years and I've gotten to know the owner, a guy named Ezra Wanton. I personally think the guy is a little dicey, you know..." Lew stopped, moved still closer to Marge and quietly whispered, "organized crime."

"Lew, we shouldn't deal with people like that," Marge responded, her voice going up an octave with fear.

"I hear ya, hon, but when I saw this opportunity I knew I could make it happen. I'd worked with Wanton before he owned the bank. He was aggressive to say the least, but mostly greedy. So... I spoke with him about FAS. I already knew Wanton was looking for another business to control and I thought Frank's business would be a perfect fit."

Lew stared at Marge for her reaction. It wasn't good. Undaunted, he went on, "So before Alice leaves Florida, I'm going to convince her that she should call Wanton and set up a meeting. Alice has always been greedy too and if she believed that there was a lucrative financial agreement for the business through Wanton, she'd jump at the chance. Once she does, I've pre-arranged a little something with Wanton so that we get a piece of the action. Win-win for me and the firm, but mostly win for us." Lew was proud of himself. He grinned at Marge like he had just swallowed Tweety bird.

Marge huffed at Lew to show her disapproval. "I don't want to go to jail, Lew. You're positive we won't get into trouble?"

"Trouble? What could possibly go wrong?"

# chapter 11

ALICE BARGED THROUGH HER front door, dropped her bags on the foyer floor and let out a long 'I'm finally home' sigh. She was glad to be back home from their vacation. More accurately she was ecstatic to be far away from Lew and Marge. They were a bore and never seemed to get anything right. Now that she was home, she intended to purposefully avoid everything and everyone, including Frank. The time she spent with him in Florida had been like taking care of a child with a constant need for attention. This was her first chance to relax a little and feel good about all that she had accomplished.

As her first order of business, Alice decided that a hot bath complete with bubbles and a tall glass of wine was an absolutely necessity. She locked the bathroom door and eased herself into the tub. The warmth of the water felt calming as it swirled around her and created clouds of steam that instantly turned the bath into her own personal sauna. She exhaled deeply, closed her eyes and completely fell into dreamland. She smiled to herself as she envisioned all the riches that would soon be hers.

As Alice finished her glass of wine, she considered Lew's advice about calling the banker, Ezra Wanton. Lew's comments seemed sincere when he stressed that she should think of herself first and finalize plans to unload that cumbersome business as soon as possible. He said an early agreement with Wanton would undoubtedly come with a sizable cash advance. He empathized that she had endured enough and this would be a great first step to her financial independence—really Alice, shouldn't you be happy too?

Alice agreed that the time was right for her to get her due. As soon as her tub cooled and her personal spa treatment concluded, she made the call. Not surprisingly, Ezra was available and had time to see her the following morning.

Alice arrived at Wanton's office fashionably late for her 10 o'clock appointment at 11:15. When she got off the elevator, she was warmly greeted by a well-built man who introduced himself as Mr. Fix.

"So nice of you to visit us today, Mrs. Strong. Mr. Wanton is available and awaiting your visit. Please come this way." Alice followed Mr. Fix down the hall into Wanton's office. All this concern over her made her feel important. She enjoyed being treated like a person of means. It was something she yearned for her entire life, something she believed she deserved.

Ever since her alcoholic parents dumped Alice and Lew into the foster system, Alice fully believed that someday she would become wealthy. Unfortunately, her dreams would never be fulfilled and Alice soon learned that if she wanted something badly enough she had to fight for it. By the time she was old enough to support herself, she accepted the fact that she would do almost anything for money.

It was in one of those dollars-for-favors cocktail bars that Alice found her true calling and where she first met Frank. She had been 'dating' other men for only a short time when Frank rambled into the bar after a grueling business trip. Frank was restlessly lonely and Alice was on the prowl for the perfect sugar daddy. As soon as they had their first drink together, she knew he was the one who would fulfill all her worldly dreams. Moreover, she knew he couldn't possibly resist her. Men craved what Alice offered and Frank was merely a man. After an evening together, Alice was certain that Frank would follow wherever she led. Now, after years of life with Frank and his unruly kids, she was excited about today's meeting. She knew it would be the culmination of her life-long effort.

"Is there anything I could get for you, Mrs. Strong?" Fix asked.

"I'm good," purred Alice as she sat and turned her attention to Ezra. He stared at her from behind his desk as he extinguished his cigarette into an overfilled ashtray.

"Please call me Ezra, all my friends do." He smiled at Mr. Fix. They both knew he had no friends. "I understand we may have a business opportunity that you would like to discuss today. Something that could be mutually beneficial? Your brother was unclear as to what you had in mind. But if the deal is right, my bank stands ready to invest."

After Ezra's brief banking introduction, Alice eyed him for a moment. She needed a minute to size him up. She wasn't comfortable enough to lay out her conspiracy idea but, at the same time, she wanted to entice Wanton. She moved to the edge of her chair to get closer. She thought if she spoke softly her message would have more impact. It sounded better that way when she had rehearsed it. Alice cautiously whispered, "I've been around Frank's business long enough to know where it's vulnerable. I know when to strike and how to make it really hurt." Alice gave herself another moment as she eyed Ezra. "I also know how to make it very very profitable." She smiled at Ezra because she knew he was interested. Still, she wouldn't divulge important details until she was sure of what she would get in return. She straightened in her chair and boldly stated, "Before we get too far into this, I want to know what's in it for me. If I do this, we must become partners, 50/50."

"Of course, Alice, I agree. That's so generous to offer us a partnership. We want you to be totally comfortable." Ezra lit another cigarette, shot a knowing glance at Mr. Fix and readied himself for Alice's plot. "When you're comfortable enough to proceed, go ahead and tell us what's on your mind," Ezra slyly enticed.

Alice's demeanor had become more laid back as she ate up Ezra's attention. She sat back, relaxed into the overstuffed armchair and began. "The idea is pretty simple actually and will take little effort from your bank."

She eyed Ezra and knew he was interested, but she waited to divulge her idea. She thought he'd want it more if he waited for it. Just as Ezra's patience was about to run out, she continued. "A short time ago, FAS took out a monster sized loan. They used the cash to purchase loads of product from their Chinese affiliate which'll be used to fulfill the next six months of sales. As you already know, collateral is always required to secure every loan. With this year's giant loan, Rick and Dylan decided to borrow as much as the bank would allow. The bank required they put up their building, machinery and inventory as collateral. It was risky, but to date their plan has worked. They've ordered the product, it's been produced and is on its way or maybe it's already arrived." She paused a moment and closed her eyes as she dramatically continued, "I know a way that we can steal the business as well as secure the entire shipment from China for about ten cents on the dollar."

Ezra smiled and leaned forward as he said, "I like where this is going and I know exactly what we should do. A few little corporate alterations between us and a bit of damning paperwork that gives the appearance FAS is guilty of some kind of banking fraud. Once their bank sees fraud, they'll go ballistic and shut FAS down by calling in their loan." Ezra gloated. "Is that about what you had in mind, Alice?"

"Exactly… As long as I get paid," Alice said.

Ezra studied Alice and confided, "Alice, as soon as you came in and sat down, I felt we were alike and that we would become fast friends. I like your idea, I like it a lot. Let's do this, let's take it all from them." Ezra reached out his sweaty hand for Alice to shake.

She sat up and reached for Ezra's hand. Before they touched, Alice demanded clarification and assurances. She reiterated, "To be absolutely clear, I get two point five million after the doors at FAS are shuttered. And, in return, you get the company, their machinery and all that product that came in from China. Right?" Alice took Ezra's hand and held it as she looked him in the eye.

"Agreed. I'll have the papers to you no later than five today," Ezra assured. He watched Alice closely as she prepared to leave. He then asked, "I need to know what to expect from the Strong boys. They certainly aren't going to hold still for this. How will they react under pressure? Do they have any weak spots?" Ezra probed.

Alice thought for a minute and said, "I'm tellin' you right now that they're a handful. But if you really want to know what they're made of, I've got a story that actually happened to them when they were kids. It's a good example of their character."

"Go ahead… tell me who they are," Ezra responded. "I certainly don't want to underestimate them."

Alice sat down and started her story. "One hot summer morning, Dylan, Rick and four other little vandals broke into a new home that was under construction in our neighborhood. All six of them crawled up into the attic through a kid-sized hole over the space that was cut out for the oven. The boys were up there smoking cigarettes when the building foreman stormed into the place and smelled the smoke. He raised holy hell and screamed at them to come down. After hearing an angry adult scream, the kids panicked—except Rick and Dylan. Without concern or hesitation, Dylan went down first through the only exit. With his feet barely past the opening, the foreman reached out and grabbed him by an ankle. He squeezed hard and yelled that he was going to take this one to the cops. Dylan fought to break free from the man's grip. But when Dylan realized the guy wouldn't let go, Dylan raised his free foot and came down hard on the man's wrist and broke his grip. The guy screamed in pain as he let go. The other kids were scared out of their little minds and thought they'd be caught as they scampered down from the attic. But Dylan stayed behind and led each of those little twerps to safe exits. Rick came down last, turned himself in to the foreman and took all the heat for all his friends. He never ratted on any of them."

Alice looked at Ezra as she concluded, "That's who they are, physically tough and mentally tougher. Times two."

"And how about their weaknesses? They must have some weaknesses." Ezra pressed. "I need something to put pressure on them."

"Friends. They treat them like gold. If you want to hurt the boys, go after their friends. That will hurt them the most."

With business concluded, Mr. Fix held open the door and gave Alice a toothy smile as she walked past him on her way to the elevator. As the doors of the elevator closed, Fix returned to Ezra's side and said, "This isn't like you, boss. I thought you would never take on a partner."

Ezra stared at his closed office door and fumed. "Partner? Before I give away two point five million dollars... my partner will suffer from an unfortunate accident that ends her miserable little life."

# chapter **12**

IT WAS MID SEPTEMBER and there was a coolness to the rain as it fell. I always felt that there were never enough warm days in Chicago. As the weather changed, Dylan and I shifted our workouts indoors and often played racquetball with our banker friend, Jeff Kim. Usually when the three of us got together for a high-energy workout, we played a variation called cutthroat. In that game one guy serves the ball and tries to score points against the combination of the other two defending players. After an intense hour of two on one, we're exhausted and warmed to the bone. Cutthroat was our personal version of Thunderdome; three go in and only one comes out the winner. It's damn fun and Jeff always won.

Our business relationship with Jeff went way back to when Dylan and I first joined the company. Jeff's in-depth knowledge of banking regulations and corporate finance allowed us to do more and grow faster than we thought possible. He's a brilliant guy, our corporate banking liaison at Loyalty National Bank and a very good friend to both of us.

This year, with Jeff's help, our company finalized a huge loan with Loyalty for five million dollars. We put up everything we had as collateral to secure it. The entire loan was used to purchase product from our Chinese affiliate overseas. With this single order, we would satisfy all of our current client needs and replenish our shelves with product. On the dock in Seattle, the shipment was due to us in a few weeks. The loan was a reach for us financially. But once the product is delivered, Dylan will do his sales magic, product will fly off the shelves and the loan will be fully repaid.

Today started strangely because Jeff was in my office for an unexpected visit. He appeared somber even though he was usually one of the most upbeat, energetic guys that Dylan and I knew. Something had to be out of place.

I watched as Jeff sat uncomfortably and shifted left to right in his chair. He seemed distant and distracted when I asked, "Hey Jeff, you good? We heard that the product is due in soon." He didn't respond and I started to get concerned. "Tell me what's going on, Jeff. Why the surprise visit?"

"Rick," Jeff said in a measured tone, "you've always been straight with me, right?"

"Absolutely, bud." I got up and moved to the chair next to him. "Come on Jeff, we're friends, tell me what's on your mind."

"We've got a real problem here, so I'm just going to come out with it. You need to listen and give me a straight answer." Jeff's voice became officious as he continued, "Late yesterday, my bank received notification that an application was filed by your company to secure another loan," Jeff stopped and looked for my reaction. I know that I must have looked startled because I had no idea what he was talking about or where this was coming from. He restarted and now spoke as if he read a prepared statement. "Loyalty National Bank has received information that a loan application was filed with Wanton Bank. It clearly indicates that FAS Inc. has applied for a cash payment of five hundred thousand dollars. In return, FAS offered its building and in-house inventory as collateral. Loyalty National wants to know if this was true."

Without waiting for a response, Jeff continued, "You already knew that your collateral was tied up with that mammoth loan you received from us. You also knew that by attempting to reuse that collateral prior to our loan repayment constituted a breach of the terms of our contract—a breach of our trust. This blatant manipulation can't go on. We won't allow it. So here's what is going to happen, Rick. This afternoon at 2pm, you and Dylan are going to be at Loyalty to meet with Bob Rend, your loan officer. Either you find a solution to this problem or..." Jeff paused. "Or Loyalty National Bank will be forced to call in your entire loan."

Jeff audibly exhaled. He was obviously stressed that he was the one who was forced to deliver the bad news. Now less officious, Jeff asked me as his friend, "Did you really do this? He paused, took a long breath and then asked. "Are you completely crazy? Do you have any idea how bad this is?"

I sat stunned as I considered these allegations, "Another loan, from another bank? No, Jeff we didn't do that!" I responded. "Why would FAS take out another loan? For what? And from some bank I've never heard of. Really, Jeff, we wouldn't do that. We didn't do that. This must be a mistake."

"Fine, you didn't do it. But the application was filed, signatures were on it and to the bank it looks like fraud." Jeff got up. "You don't screw your friends, Rick." Without another word, Jeff left my office.

I stared blindly at my door and tried to think. If we applied for any loan, my signature had to be on it or it simply couldn't have happened. Our corporate bylaws clearly state that an officer's signature must appear on every document as a safeguard. Who would be so stupid to purposefully mess with our company? I jumped up and screamed, "Dylan, where the hell is Dad?"

Dylan ran to my office. "What's going on Rick?"

I repeated the details of my conversation with Jeff. Dylan couldn't believe this had happened as he stood silent at my doorway.

"Dylan, why would he do this? For Christ sake, how did he do this? After his last episode, he was under observation. How could he have convinced a bank to give him money?"

"Hell, in his condition most people wouldn't give him the time of day," Dylan chided. After he thought for a minute, Dylan harshly asked, "Wasn't it your job to get his name off the corporate papers by now?"

"Coulda, shoulda, woulda ain't helpin' right now Dylan!" I flared as I became more agitated.

"Then tell me how our incapacitated dad did all this and where he is right now!" demanded Dylan.

"D, the last I heard, Alice and Dad just got back from their annual fun in the sun vacation with brother Lew. But, Dylan, it couldn't have been Dad. Let's face it, he doesn't have the mental capacity anymore to pull off something this complicated. He's just a sick old man. Alice had to put him up to this. Just sayin'."

"I think you're right, Rick, but we can't fix what we don't know. We've got to find him." Dylan went to his office to start his search.

After repeated calls and emails messages, it became abundantly clear to me that neither Alice or Dad would respond. I called Mary into my office. She brought coffee and sat in front of my desk.

"I'm here to help, boss," Mary said. "What's up?"

I grinned but when I responded I must have sounded worried when I said, "We've got a problem. Someone is out there coming at us and I'm not sure who it is. But we've got to stop them."

Mary looked at me and flashed her beautiful movie star smile as she calmly stated, "Then we will stop them." She straightened and went on, "And... I'm confident we'll succeed cuz I believe in you. I feel certain that together we can fix anything."

My entire attitude skyrocketed. I sat up and smiled back at her. "Then young lady, you'd better get busy too. I need you to reach out to everyone you know and get everything there is on Wanton Bank. If we're going to beat these guys, we'd better get smarter right now."

# chapter 13

"RICK AND DYLAN STRONG to see Bob Rend, we have a two o'clock," I said to Lily West, the receptionist at Loyalty National Bank. Loyalty had been our company's corporate bank since Dad first started selling hard metal brake pads. They've always been in our corner and had backed us financially on more than one occasion.

"Please have a seat. Bob will be with you in a minute." Lily said as she smiled at Dylan and pointed to the waiting area. I started in the direction that Lily had indicated but Dylan stayed behind. He wanted a little more face time with Lily, a former bikini model and current love interest. The two of them dated several times and seemed to be getting closer.

I've never been good at waiting and today was no exception. Within minutes after I sat down, my back began to ache and it became abundantly clear to me that this chair was created by some sadistic interior designer who went all-in for style and hated comfort. But after I exhaled and reconsidered, I realized the chair was probably fine and that I was super nervous. Dylan sensed my anxiety as he came over and sat next to me. He tapped my arm with a rolled magazine and said, "After Bob agrees with us, things will go back to normal. Sound good?"

I usually don't hear the calm voice from Dylan but he was spot on. "You're right. The bank'll back us. We've done a ton of business together. Econ101 says that they'll always do better with us than without us, right?" I rambled.

Our meeting was with newly named Vice President, Bob Rend. Bob was also our loan officer and he had approved this year's loan. After I called this morning, Bob had agreed to see us, if only to tell us how incredibly screwed our corporate finances had become. We completely understood that this conversation could determine if our little company would be allowed to survive. We were sure that some of the fallout from this must have rubbed off on Bob. For all of these reasons, Dylan and I were there on time, dressed appropriately, and on our best behavior.

"Rick, Dylan, come in," Bob said without expression. He half-heartedly held out his hand for us to shake and quickly guided us into his office. As we walked, Bob was quiet and his mood was obviously cold.

Once in his office and the door closed, Bob wasted no time getting to the point. His demeanor went from cold to totally confrontational when he asked, "Tell me how you planned to get away with this?"

With each word, Bob's anger grew. "I'm positive Loyalty National has gone out of its way to be good to FAS Inc. Hell, I've personally gone miles out of my way to be good to you two. But, your recent actions in regards to this loan—I've gotta tell you guys and I'm not speaking for just myself when I say—it pisses me off, dammit."

By now Bob's voice was nearing full yell as he continued to berate Dylan and me. "I personally signed off on that loan. Do you have any idea what this is going to do to my career? Do either of you care? If you've got something to say in your defense, say it now."

Bob sat motionless and glared at us. I knew he expected us to spout some sort of smart-aleck response. Not today. I saw how upset he was. I wanted to calmly explain what had happened from our point of view.

"Mr. Rend," I started cautiously. "In our defense, this entire situation was a complete surprise. Our first and only indication of any wrongdoing was when Jeff Kim visited us this morning. When he told me that there was a second loan application, we were totally floored. Neither Dylan nor I requested any loan of any bank and would have never tried to defraud Loyalty. We believe that this unfortunate situation must somehow be tied to our dad. Over the last couple years, he's become a bit demented and has done some very odd things. Since Jeff's visit, we've tried every way possible to contact him, but he hasn't responded. Mr. Rend, we are honestly unsure of what has transpired."

Once I finished my lame excuses, I examined Bob's reaction. It wasn't good.

"So you're telling me that you're not responsible because your demented old man was the one who attempted to defraud this bank? And allegedly you know nothing about how or why he did it?"

Bob ran his hand over his eyes, scowled at us and angrily restarted, "Fraud is what this looks like to me, Rick. Fraud, plain and simple. For one minute did you believe that Loyalty National wouldn't know? What kind of idiots do you think we are?"

"Mr. Rend, Bob," Dylan said as he interceded for me in the conversation. "We feel terrible this occurred. We really do. Our company has deep roots in this community, just like this bank. We continue to be loyal to only this bank. Whatever has happened, we have been an unwitting accomplice in someone else's unethical game. Bob, we need your help to uncover the truth. We have always trusted and relied on the security that you've provided to us through Loyalty National. Please give us the time to investigate and make this right. Tell us what we can do to keep our doors open and keep our people employed. I'm positive we will get to the bottom of this. Please, sir, we just need a little time."

I stared at Dylan in total awe. I had just witnessed Dylan Strong in ultra-sales mode as he completely mesmerized Bob Rend. That eloquent speech was something to behold.

Bob relaxed behind his desk and reopened our file. He actually took another look! We watched as he ran through the columns of data and then said, "It looks like the product is in port and could deliver to your facility in as little as two weeks—if we decide to release the final funds. Let me take a look...." Bob stroked his goatee while he contemplated. He closed the file folder and laid it back on his desk, looked up at us and said, "Here's what I expect. I want signed letters of intent from buyers for every bit of the new product. And no payments of any sort to anyone can go out until this matter is completely cleared up. None. That includes employee payroll."

Dylan and I looked at each other and nodded our agreement to Bob's demands. We could talk to our buyers to convince them to do as Bob had asked and Dylan and I would cover payroll ourselves until this was over. Dylan did a few fast calculations and thought that it would take the better part of two weeks to get all the documents back to Bob. "We could do this," Dylan replied. "Would you allow us just a couple weeks?"

"You still don't seem to fully understand," Bob said. "If FAS doesn't end its business with Wanton immediately, Loyalty National expects the return of our entire five million dollars in five business days. To make that absolutely clear, the funds are due next week Thursday by end of day or we take the building, the property and all of the new product."

"Bob, that's why we've come to you today. Can't you give us an extension of just a couple more days?" Dylan pleaded.

"Jesus, Dylan, I don't have to give you two anything. I could have called in your damn loan today!" Bob gave us one last exasperated look and walked to his office door. As he held it open for Dylan and me, he gave one last bit of advice. "I don't think you fully comprehend your real problem boys. It's Wanton. You'd better deal with him soon, before its too late. And remember boys, Thursday, close of business."

As Dylan and I crossed through the bank's lobby, he flashed one of his toothy smiles and cooed, "Easy peasy, brother. We got this." He put his arm around my shoulder and continued, "Rick, we'll deal with that other bank soon enough. But agree with me or don't, things could have been a lot worse."

"You're right, D, but I've got this weird feeling that things are going get a lot worse."

My phone buzzed and I realized that I could tell the future.

"Hello, Rick, this is Ezra Wanton, Wanton Bank. We need to get together and discuss our new business arrangements."

# chapter **14**

EARLY THE NEXT MORNING, Mary stood on the street in front of the police department's electronic surveillance unit (ESU). The building was headquarters for the city's newest top secret high-tech crime prevention unit. They were responsible for digital threat assessment and evaluation including city-wide electronic surveillance. Basically, they looked for trouble before it happened to anyone or anything everywhere in the city. Once they found a potential threat, it was instantly linked to the major crimes task force for fast resolution. Since inception, the accuracy of their assessments was amazing and probably one major reason for the steep drop in the crime rate. The surveillance unit worked quietly in the shadows to maintain its complete anonymity. There was no reason to brag about its investigative excellence.

Mary's cousin Detective Vinny DeMano worked at ESU. He surveilled internet conversations from one bad guy to another. Vinny always quipped, "What the bad guys thought was secret usually isn't anymore."

Mary was well known by many of the officers in the building. Every Monday morning for the first two months that Vinny worked in surveillance, Mary brought in a basket full of fresh blueberry muffins for the squad. Mary wanted to do what she could to help her cousin, maybe even help further his career. He was family after all. Nothin' you wouldn't do for family.

Vinny looked up from his monitor as Mary approached. He got up immediately and gave her a warm hug as he quietly confided, "Ever since you brought in all those muffins, the guys here in the squad room have been callin' me Blueberry." Vinny smiled at Mary and went on, "Wanna know somethin'... I kinda like it."

Vinny moved some files off the chair next to his desk and directed Mary to sit. He asked, "Hey, Mary? Lately I only see you when you need something. What's up with that?"

"Why Detective DeMano, what are you sayin'?" Mary smiled and tried to look coy. "Now that you mention it, there is a little … something … that I need to find out about."

"I can't give you information, Mary. You already know that," Vinny scolded. He looked over his shoulders, then back to Mary as he said in low tones, "If you're havin' a problem, remember that me and the other guys are here for you. You got that, right? I'm a cop and you're my cousin for cry eye." He looked at Mary; she still had a look that told Vinny she needed something. Vinny rubbed his eyes and said in hushed tones, "OK, Mary, I can look up stuff but you gotta stay in that chair. I can't let you look at the screen. It's policy."

Mary nodded her approval. "Thanks, Vin. The guy's name is Ezra Wanton." She spelled out Ezra's last name. "What can you tell me about this dude?"

Vinny typed in the name and read his monitor. His eyes grew big as saucers as he looked at the information on his screen. "What the hell, Mary? What are you doing with this guy? He's dangerous."

"Vin, I don't know all the details, but I do know that the guy screwed with my bosses and we've got to know who we're fighting," she replied. "Can I see the file? Just for a sec?"

"Mary, no, we already went over that. All I can tell you is that the department has an open case file on this guy and all this information is sealed. Sorry, but not today, Mary," Vinny firmly but apologetically answered.

Mary acted upbeat and said, "Thanks anyhow, Vinny. I totally understand. It's your job after all."

Mary looked around the room while she readied herself to leave and asked, "You still coming to dinner Saturday? I'm makin' pot roast and boiled potatoes. We need to talk soon about what you're bringin'." Mary got up from her chair and hugged Vinny goodbye as he sat in front of his monitor. She turned back to him and sweetly asked, "Vin, is it alright if I take a selfie with you? I don't have any photos of us together in your new office." Without waiting for his reply, Mary took out her cell, raised it as the two of them smiled and took the shot. "Love ya Vin, see ya Saturday." Mary stuffed her phone into her purse and hurried out of his office.

"See ya Saturday," he replied. He looked back at his monitor and realized what she had done.

Mary quickly exited, got into her car and took out her cell. She opened the selfie and saw Vinny, herself and a clear image of Vinny's monitor with all of Ezra's data. She quickly put the phone back into her purse and sped back to the office.

It didn't take long for Mary to pull together the information. She joined the meeting in Rick's office and immediately started into what she had found. "My first observation of Ezra Wanton is that this guy likes to live on the edge."

Dylan interrupted her and said, "Come on, Mary, everyone has a skeleton or two in their closet. A little indiscretion isn't so far out of the norm. Don't you have anything concrete that we can use against him?"

Mary quietly fumed and shot Dylan one of those 'I'm not finished' looks. She stared at Dylan as she took an elongated sip of her cola and restarted with a touch of pretentiousness. "If everyone would please hold off on all of their premature, unwanted commentary until after my presentation. Thank you very much."

Dylan sat back on the office sofa and pretended to zip his lips shut as he said 'sorry' with his mouth closed.

A stack of papers lay in front of Mary. On each sheet she had scribbled cryptic notations. Mary shuffled through the pile and reorganized a few sheets. When she was ready, she started to rhythmically unfold the life of Ezra Wanton.

"I got most of this information from my cousin Vinny. He's with the cyber division now. Don't ask how I got this stuff cause it may not be legal."

She began, "Seems that Ezra started out like any other kid. Normal family—mom, dad, one sister. Everything seemed fine until the night before his eighth birthday when his parents died from smoke inhalation during a house fire as they slept."

"Kid do it?" Dylan asked.

"Unknown."

"Still, that must have been rough," I added.

We listened as Mary peeled back the layers. "His sister wound up in a bad foster care home and died of pneumonia when she was only ten. Ezra never had the chance to see her or say goodbye." Mary paused as her eyes welled a little with tears. She went on, "After that, he was bounced from place to place but nothing seemed to work out for him. When he was fourteen, he walked away from his foster family and didn't return. No one even bothered to look for him. There doesn't seem to be any gang affiliation but there were charges filed against him for grand theft auto when he was eighteen. He liked fast cars. The case was dropped after the owner of the stolen car was severely beaten shortly before the trial and suddenly developed amnesia. When Ezra was in his twenties there were allegations that he worked for a loan shark as their collection muscle. Word is, he liked to inflict pain. He got caught and before he went to trial the charges were also magically dropped."

"Seems Ezra has a sketchy history," Dylan said with a shrug.

Mary stopped reading. "Aren't you listening? This guy is scary and he can hurt us. Don't screw around."

Mary continued as she glossed over Ezra's criminal highlights, "He's a hustler, a con man, a card cheat; the list goes on. I found information that suggested Ezra may have been directly involved in the death of the last bank president, James Folan. The document indicated that prior to the Wanton takeover, Mr. Folan was 'accidentally' killed as he came home from church. The following week, Ezra somehow gained control of the bank, fired most of the top executives and moved himself into the corner office. There's more. Ezra was listed as the only 'person of interest' in last year's unsolved murder of Judge Jonas Fairman, but the cops haven't found anyone who was willing to testify against him. Guys, this dude is crazy and dangerous."

"Thanks, Mary," I said. "We won't underestimate him."

"You had better not," Mary demanded as she pointed at both Dylan and me, "because at 3 o'clock this afternoon, you both have an appointment downtown at the Wanton Bank. A limo will be here at 2."

"Could have led with that Mary, just sayin'." I checked the time and realized the limo would be at our door in just a few minutes. I grabbed my list of Wanton questions from my desk and jammed them into my pocket and asked Dylan, "What do you expect out of this meeting?"

Dylan looked at me as he straightened his tie, "The dude had better tell us why the hell he's screwing with us."

"I just hope it doesn't get ugly," I said to myself.

# chapter **15**

AT EXACTLY TWO O'CLOCK the Wanton stretch limo arrived. Two beefy gorillas dressed in well-tailored Brooks Brothers suits got out. Dylan gave them a look and said to me, "This Ezra guy has got some big friends. Think they want something to eat? They look hungry."

I glared at Dylan as we walked past the behemoths and got into the limo. I was proud to see that Dylan didn't purposefully antagonize these guys and make more enemies. Good boy, Dylan.

The ride in the limo brought back memories of when we were kids and rode with Dad. He taught us that limos gave your opposition an edge. He said that when he drove a client in his car, he recorded every one of their conversations. On more than one occasion he used those conversations for his benefit. As we drove downtown to Wanton's, we expected that Ezra had done the same. To screw with him, Dylan and I filled the drive time arguing about the rules of cutthroat racquetball. Dylan believed that the server should be allowed to bump an opponent when they are trying to make a shot. I disagreed, total interference. The argument lasted the entire trip. We wouldn't give Ezra any information unless we wanted him to have it.

Regardless of traffic, our monsters of the roadway got us to our destination on-time. We stepped out of the limo in front of Wanton's building a hair before 3pm. Our chauffeur, Ugly the Giant, rolled down his window and scowled at us as he grunted, "Seventh floor, Room 723." What a guy.

The Wanton Bank building was old—like it had been built before electricity was invented—old. The lobby also preserved this well-worn design. Most of the furniture was built in the 1960's; it was unmanned, unused and smelled like mildew. Even the ancient elevator was reluctant to act as it creaked and jerked throughout its painful ascent. This wasn't what we expected from a successful bank.

As soon as Dylan and I stepped onto the seventh floor, we were met by a well-dressed man who called himself Mr. Fix. This one wasn't a gorilla and he didn't wear a fake smile. He was average height, built strongly and moved like a fighter. His deep-set cold eyes made him appear dangerous. When I noticed that he holstered a gun under his jacket, I knew he was the gate keeper, Ezra Wanton's bodyguard. "Good afternoon, gentlemen. Mr. Wanton is expecting you. Follow me."

I pulled back on Dylan's arm and said into his ear, "Careful, D, I think this guy wants to play rough."

Dylan nodded and kept an eye on Mr. Fix. We both had a gut feeling that sooner or later we would be forced to deal with him. If this meeting went south, it certainly would be sooner.

Mr. Fix opened the door to Suite 723 and directed Dylan and me inside. He slipped in behind us and slithered into a darkened corner.

Ezra's office was dark and warm. Not a good kind of warm; it had to be eighty degrees in the room. The space was filled with overstuffed furniture in an ancient art deco style which gave it a distinct garage sale vibe. Every window was covered with heavy brown curtains. The room's only illumination came from two small lamps which sat on either side of Ezra's oversized wooden desk. The smell of old cigarettes and dust was everywhere. We stepped in and waited for our eyes to adjust to the dim light.

A slightly pudgy, balding man in his mid-fifties stepped out from behind the desk. My first impression of this guy didn't scream psycho killer. I thought he acted more like a regular guy—kind of killer.

"Thanks so much for taking the time to come visit with me," Ezra said. "I've heard so many things about you two. Alice has been very forthcoming." He fixed his glare on us and tried to determine from our reactions if what Alice had said was at all real. There was no change in our expressions. We were there to listen and learn, not play into Ezra's traps.

"Rick, Dylan, let's relax a minute," he started as he smiled to himself and acted like it was a struggle to hide some secret. "I'd like to talk for a while before I give you guys all the answers," he said, still fighting back something he thought amusing. Ezra pulled a pack of Marlboro's out of his jacket. "Want one? Oh, not your brand?" He smirked as he tapped the end of his cigarette on his desk to more tightly pack the tobacco. He lit up, inhaled deeply and blew out a stream of smoke into the air. Still amused by something invisible on his ceiling, he smiled to himself and slowly said, "What a story, what a story I have got for the two of you."

Ezra took a long moment and examined both Dylan and me. He took another deep drag on his smoke. "Rick, Dylan... I've gotta say that Alice is quite a piece of work, isn't she? Never mind answering, we all already know," he said with a wave of his hand and another drag on his smoke. Ezra eyed us as he asked, "You don't have any idea what's going to happen to FAS Inc., do you?"

"Going to happen to our company?" I replied. "Nothing. That's what's going to happen, absolutely nothing."

Ezra began to respond when an impatient Dylan harshly interjected, "Enough of this nonsense, Ezra. Just come out with it and tell us why you dragged us downtown."

"Sure thing, Dylan. I thought you'd be the one to appreciate the drama. I'll get right to it so try to relax and I'll lay it out for both of you."

I could see that Ezra enjoyed the thought of what was coming as he wiggled his ass in his seat to sink in deeper. He took another deep drag and blew out a plume of smoke as he began, "A short time ago your loving stepmother approached me with an intriguing thought. Her idea was simple and required only a little paperwork. So, together we created a limited partnership corporation comprised of your business FAS Inc. and Wanton Bank. It took almost nothing for Alice to coerce Frank to sign it all away. Among the many forms he signed was one for a small start-up loan. To secure that loan, Frank put up his building and inventory as collateral. Really guys, he couldn't have possibly remembered that he used that same asset for your current unpaid loan."

Ezra stopped and sucked on his smoke again. After he exhaled in my direction, he grinned and continued, "The real easy part was for Wanton Bank to simply file the application in all the right places with all the right agencies to make sure it got noticed. And did it ever get noticed. Loyalty National Bank called almost immediately looking for details. After that, we sat back and enjoyed watching your financial world as it swirled round and round."

"This is all bullshit," Dylan dismissed.

"Not true, Dylan, not true at all," Ezra said. "It was all made possible because Alice had already taken control of the company from Frank. He may not have completely understood what he signed, but Frank turned over everything to Alice—I personally witnessed as he signed the paperwork. And boys, if that's not enough to piss you off, your beloved stepmom and Wanton Bank have completed and signed an agreement that gave me, Wanton Ltd., controlling interest of FAS Inc." As Ezra finished, he felt content enough to flash his uneven yellowed smile.

It took me a while, but I finally realized that the only reason we were in his office was for him to gloat. He wanted to watch us squirm over his nasty news. I wouldn't give him the pleasure and remained calm as I said, "We'll deal with Alice later. Why don't you tell us exactly what you get out of this? What's in it for you?"

Ezra shook his head and laughed to himself again. "Still not seeing the big picture yet, are ya, Richie? Then let me make this real simple for the slower kids in the front row." Ezra purposefully slowed his speech as he condescendingly continued, "FAS currently has tons of product sitting on a dock in Seattle. I want that product. To keep the new product out of your hands, we released information that made it appear FAS Inc. had illegally manipulated collateral previously used to secure a huge loan. We fully expected Loyalty National would call in your loan, which you won't be able to pay back." Ezra stopped long enough to suck on his cigarette. After an elongated exhale, he looked directly at me. "Five mil is a bitch to instantly make appear, isn't it Richie?"

The pudgy bastard giggled. "Without the cash, FAS closes down and Loyalty is forced to take receipt of all that new product sitting on the docks in Seat-tle." Ezra enjoyed our bewilderment. "Still with me, sluggers? Good… cuz here's the really sexy part. Once Loyalty takes control of the product, a shell company of Wanton will contact them and want to purchase that unclaimed new product at a severely reduced cost. My guess… ten cents on the dollar. Loyalty gets a win by unloading a bad asset and I win by taking receipt of five—million—dollars' worth of new product, ultra cheap. With the new product comes the building, machinery and everything else. Bottom line, boys… FAS Inc. is mine."

"Not going to happen, Ezzie," Dylan yelled as he pointed at Wanton.

"Time to wake the hell up, boys. It's already hap-pened." Ezra raised his voice and called out, "Mr. Fix, please show these gentlemen the door." Ezra sucked on his cigarette and blew the smoke my way. "Stop by again… anytime."

We took the limo back to the office, this time in complete silence.

# chapter 16

I SAT AT MY desk and blindly stared at Dylan as I replayed yesterday's meeting with Wanton. It couldn't have gone worse. So many ill fitting pieces were arranged by Alice and signed by Dad. That wasn't possible. He wouldn't have ever done anything to hurt us and she's not smart enough. We needed to find him immediately.

Dylan stayed angry and fixated on Alice as he mused aloud about how he wanted to stuff her into a suitcase and ship her to a third world country.

"Not helpin', D," I said. "Let's focus on constructive solutions, please."

"Sure, Rick, but let's first agree that the bitch was responsible. I'm positive Alice conned Dad into thinking that he was helping us or at minimum helping the company when he signed those papers. That would explain why all this crap has happened."

"That's all fine, D. Alice was responsible. We agree. Happy? But remember that Dad's still the key. Once we find him, we'll get answers. We've already burned through the first day the bank gave us and we're still no closer to straightening this out."

I impatiently looked around the room and finally back at Dylan as I said, "I've called all of Dad's usual haunts and some of the more unusual ones, but I got nada. Unless you've got a better idea, I think we should take a ride to his house. Maybe Alice hid him in the basement or something."

We were on the road in five and in front of Dad's home in less than half an hour. We rang the bell, waited and rang it again. I turned the knob expecting it to be locked but the door opened. Dylan and I yelled in unison "Anybody home?" It had been a long time since we were here last but we're family, no one would mind if we went in. I yelled again as we entered the house and started to look around, "Anybody? Anybody? Buehler?"

"We know he's back from Florida. Where would you stash him if you were Alice?" I asked. I caught up to Dylan as he searched dad's computer. "Find anything?"

"Oh Jesus!" shrieked Dylan as he leaped out of the chair. "There are pictures of her in there... naked! I'll never be able to unsee that." Dylan huffed as he threw the mouse away like it was infected with the Ebola virus."Friggin' Alice."

"Friggin' Alice," I replied.

My phone was set on silent, but I felt it vibrate. I saw it was Mary and answered "Family break-in service, how may we help today?" What can I say, she's into my cute thing.

I listened and heard Mary softly sobbing. "I just got a message from Alice. Your dad is at Good Savior Hospital. He's in the Emergency Room."

We were in the car in seconds and we raced to the hospital. The rain that was forecast was now coming down in buckets. The intense sound of the rain on the car roof along with the thumping of the wipers kept my mind off what we knew was to come. Neither of us spoke.

By the time we arrived Dad had already been admitted and was now in ICU. Activity was everywhere as doctors and nurses swarmed around him and administered test after test in an attempt to determine what had occurred and how to fix it. Dylan and I helicoptered from room to front desk and back to his room and continually asked for any new information about Dad's condition. It wasn't long before we were politely asked to leave the ICU and find the area down the hall to wait until results became available.

To pass the time, Dylan and I restlessly walked the linoleum hallways and drank the harsh machine coffee. We worried about Dad and thought about what the future would look like without him. Just the thought of losing him made us think of the loss of our mom.

It had been years since she had died. That was our first loss, parent or otherwise—and we were just kids when it happened. Our mom, Angie Romano Strong, had always been the sweetest, kindest, most beautiful woman ever born. There has never been a better Mom.

As Dad always put it, she was the hottest woman he'd ever seen. They had met at a concert in Grant Park, instantly fell in love and planned a large family wedding for the following spring. Mom said Frank Strong was the most confident man she had ever met. She knew he was the one, even though he was twelve years older than her.

Together they planned a giant wedding with the entire family invited. Her parents fully paid for it as their gift to the new couple. They really couldn't afford anything of that magnitude and hadn't saved nearly enough to pay for it, but they took out a loan because Angie was their first to wed and they wanted to do something special, something absolutely memorable.

With the invitations sent and the date only two months away, Frank decided that he couldn't wait any longer to be with his Angie. He argued with her and said that the ceremony was a waste of time, a family formality. He told her that they shouldn't have restrictions and should be allowed to do what they want—including being allowed to make love prior to the nuptials. He knew she couldn't, or more accurately wouldn't, agree and would remain a virgin until she tied the knot.

Frank knew he could change her mind if the circumstances were right. His opportunity arrived on the coldest day of winter after Angie had become bedridden with a high fever due to the flu that worsened and became pneumonia. Frank dismissed her condition, told her that it was just a cold and demanded that she get out of bed so that she could be his forever. He was relentless. Too feverishly weak to withstand any more arguments, Angie reluctantly acquiesced to his demands. The two were married that night by a judge at city hall. No one she knew attended the ceremony.

The news of her nuptials spread fast throughout the family. Her parents were outraged, shocked and most of all, deeply hurt. Unfortunately, they were still on the hook for the entire cost of the reception, whether it happened or not. What made things worse for Angie was that her family responded to the couple with anger. How could Frank have done such a vile thing to their Angie? And while she was sick in bed with pneumonia?

Frank became incensed by their attitude toward him because he believed he was right to do as he chose. So he doubled down and openly dismissed all of them as unimportant and unnecessary. All of which further alienated Angie from everyone she loved or cared about.

Her family situation was never resolved. Until the day that Angie died, not a single relative ever crossed their threshold. Not one birthday card or message of goodwill was ever sent. Throughout all those years, she never openly complained about the loss of her family. Our mom has been and will always be the best mom a kid could ever want.

Knowing all this, we still couldn't understand what Dad ever saw in that bitch Alice. She was cruel and uncaring. It was never more obvious as she sauntered into the waiting area from the cafeteria. Her biggest concern, believe it or not, wasn't about Dad. It was about her steak—the meat was too grizzly and undercooked. She didn't even take the time to ask about Dad's condition. Everything about Alice irritated me. Screw her.

What we really needed were the results from all the tests. They still weren't in and we surmised that they must have gotten lost somewhere between any minute now and it may be a while. The only thing that we heard about Dad was from unreliable Alice. She indicated that one of the doctors mentioned that Dad had an unbalanced heart rhythm, whatever that was supposed to be. There was never an explanation given to me from anyone on the medical staff. We were repeatedly told that information would be forthcoming shortly.

Our wait for answers wasn't long. The nurse rushed into the waiting room and confirmed our worst fears as she quickly stated, "You all had better get in there now." Her voice sounded of imminent doom. "He's failing."

Dylan and I were at his bedside instantly. Alice strolled in after she finished her magazine article and sat alone on the hard couch near the door. Dad looked uncomfortable with all the spaghetti-like arrays of wires and tubes that connected him to all the latest expensive hospital gear. I was momentarily detracted from the emergency right in front of me by all the alarms, bells and whistles that trilled around us. I noticed that each machine had its own distinctive sound and was only decipherable by the experienced nurses. They located which machine, the intensity of the emergency and without hesitation, instantly translated their analysis to the doctors for action.

Dylan and I were seated on either side of the bed and examined everything. Above the mechanical din, Dad began to ramble incoherently about things from our distant past. His breathing was labored and difficult, his color was becoming a yellowish-blue. At one point he stopped breathing altogether, then he gasped loudly, opened his eyes and saw both of his sons. A tear formed in his eye. He knew we were there for him. After all he had done we were still his blood, still his boys.

"I'm sorry," a somewhat lucid Frank stated. He cleared his throat and softly confided, "I thought I could set you both up for life. I thought it would work. Alice told me it would work." His eyes slowly closed and his breathing got shallow.

"What would work? What did Alice do?" Dylan directly questioned. "Dad? Come on, tell us something."

Hearing Dylan's plea, Dad eyes eased open as he tried his best to sit up. Uncomfortably, he spoke without looking at either of us, "I tried to make you men without letting you enjoy being boys..." he winced as he cleared his throat and went on, "I may have failed you then, but I didn't fail you now. I made sure I did something right—my last and best gift to both of you—is my will. I left you boys the business and all of my savings. I should've shared what I wanted to do sooner; I should've done a lot of things and been a better dad. I swear boys, I've always loved you both," he stopped as his face contorted terribly and showed discernible pain.

I looked over at Dylan as he held Dad's hand. With every painful wince Dad made, Dylan winced too. It looked to me like Dylan tried to take on Dad's pain. There was a loving connection between them that I hadn't ever seen. But their moment was short lived and ended abruptly when Dad's eyes rolled back and he suddenly crashed.

Alarm bells screamed out simultaneously and alerted the medical staff of Dad's bad news. Groups of doctors and nurses ran to him from all directions. They flew into Dad's room and engulfed his bed as they attempted to save him. As they worked, Dylan and I were shoved backwards until Dad was nearly out of sight. Frantically, as many as ten people worked, pumped and tried to shock him back to life. Determined, they continued to fight as they upped the wattages and increased the doses until there was nothing left that they could do to save our dad.

Time of death, 12:37 am.

Dylan and I cried and hugged each other. Our dad was gone. Alice walked out of the room as if she was late for her hair appointment.

chapter **17**

OUR WORLD CONTINUED TO spin with the loss of Dad. We weren't really sure what we should do. We thought if we met at the office we could think about what happened and determine what to do next.

We were there only a short time when Beau Reese, Dad's personal friend and attorney, stopped by to offer his respects. He and Dad had been golf buddies for over twenty-five years and he was terribly shaken by the news. We all went into the conference room, as Beau tearfully said, "Your dad was a great man, boys. He constantly bragged about you both." Beau stopped to blot his red eyes. "Frank had some ideas of his own. He hated the idea of being all dressed up and propped up in some casket. He told me, 'Don't you ever let them put me on display in a box. If you do, I'll come back and haunt you.'" Beau smiled through his tears about Dad's comment as he remembered the moment.

"Boys, your dad left me something to read to the two of you in the event of his death." Beau reached into his coat pocket and withdrew an old folded letter. He slowly unfolded it and began to read:

"If Beau is reading this letter to you boys, I must be dead. I know I could have done some things differently, but the mistakes I made should have prepared you both for your own life challenges. The rest is up to you. I want my funeral to be private, fast and without any ceremony. As soon as I pass, I want you to cremate my body. Then I want you to spread my ashes down the middle of my open fairway for as far as the eye can see. You know the place, boys. It was where I first saw what great men you both would become. I'm so damn proud to have been your dad. Remember me, boys. You were everything to me and the best parts of my life."

I cried when Beau finished. So did Dylan. Beau handed me the letter and got up to leave. We invited him to stay for some coffee. He asked for a rain check. As Beau reached the door, he said, "I'll see you both later this afternoon at my office for the reading of the will. Don't be late."

Throughout the morning there were many calls from friends and clients, all of them offering their condolences. Each of them took a minute and reminisced about how their lives intersected with Dad's. In each case we thanked them and wished them our best. Even in death people still spoke well of Dad.

I contacted Ripkin's Funeral Home and arranged the cremation Dad wanted. Outside of that, Dylan and I roamed around the office without anything that we needed or wanted to accomplish. Nothing seemed important enough to warrant our attention. Most everyone understood and if they didn't, we really didn't care. The day uneventfully dragged on.

Shortly after lunch, our day worsened when Ezra Wanton and his pet, Mr. Fix, decided to make an uninvited unwanted visit. They paraded into the office and pranced around as they tried to act important. "Nice to see that you've kept the place in working order," Ezra spouted. He reeked of stale cigarettes mixed with Old Spice. "That'll make the transition much easier."

"Wanton, we're not interested in your bullshit today. Why don't you say what you've come to say and then get the hell out." I purposefully moved into his path to cut off his meandering. "We're in no mood to play games."

"Games!? Rick, this is no game. I own this company, I own this building, hell... I own the two of you," Ezra announced as he tested my limits.

A surge of outrage passed through me as the emotion of losing Dad took over. "You think so, huh?" I said as I stepped closer to Ezra. "Would you like to personally experience how we deal with idiots who test our patience?"

Dylan turned to face Ezra's pit bull, Mr. Fix, and readied himself. "Yo, Ezzie," he said in a tone as insulting as possible. His gaze locked on Fix as he went on. "Take the leash off your dog so that I can slap the grin off its ugly face." Dylan closed the gap between himself and Fix. "I don't know about you, Rick, but right now, I feel like hurting someone. And that someone is standing right in front of me," Dylan threatened.

The two men tensed as Mr. Fix reached into his jacket and put the grip of his pistol in his hand. "You're not fast enough to get that out before I break your face, Fixie." Dylan promised.

Dylan stared into his opponent's eyes. They would foretell his next move. Everyone stood still and waited for someone to blink.

In the midst of all the tension, the office door opened and Mary barged into the room. She stopped in her tracks and glared at the four men before she began to yell, "There's no time for this crap. You and you," she said as she pointed at Wanton and Fix. "Get out! Get out now! Can't you see these boys are mourning for their dad? What's wrong with you? Don't ya know any better? Now... get out!" Mary used her hands like a broom as she attempted to sweep away the unwanted vermin.

"Are you talking to me?" asked an indignant Wanton. "I own this company! No one talks like that to me."

"Congratulations, I'm so happy for you," Mary snarled back. "Let me rephrase, GET THE HELL OUT!" Mary pointed at the door.

Ezra and Fix started to leave, but stopped at the door to say something only to have me cut them off. "We know, Ezra, this isn't the end of this. We're gonna see your ugly mug again real soon. Blah-blah-blah. Now get the hell out."

After they were gone, Mary let loose. "Are you two bozos out of your little minds? Didn't you hear me when I said that that guy is dangerous?" She moved to the window and watched. Then she looked into my eyes when she said, "Don't you realize how much I care about you two? And that I couldn't bear it if either of you got hurt. Not now, not after your dad. You know it would break my heart," Mary said as she began to cry.

I put my arm around her and tried to ease her feelings. "We love you too, Mary. We're fine. Things just got... a little crazy for a minute," I said as she walked away and dried her tears.

Dylan still looked defensive. There was definitely something that bothered him. As he came closer, he held out his hand and said quietly, "Rick, take a look at this." There was something small and electronic in his palm. He made a 'keep quiet' motion with his finger pressed to his lips.

He held up a small disc-shaped circuit board with tiny antennae on the top. It looked to me to be a listening device. Dylan closed his hand around it and put his hand in his pocket. He looked peeved. Barely audible, he said, "Do you believe him? That moron comes into our office, shows us no respect and leaves a bug? He must think we're idiots."

With his voice still hushed, Dylan asked, "Remember how Dad always told us that we should record everything and leave nothing to chance?" I nodded as I started to see where Dylan was going with this. I saw the tactical advantage as he continued, "How about we use this thing to screw with Ezzie and make him think what we want him to think?"

Dylan removed the device from his pocket and put it back where he found it. Dylan smiled as he did it because we both knew Ezra had just given us a lovely parting gift.

Mary's voice boomed over the intercom as she suddenly announced, "I just remembered... you're both supposed to be at the attorney's office right now. It's the reading of your dad's will."

# chapter 18

THE EASY DRIVE TO Beau's office was significantly slower due to more heavy rain. Torrents filled the streets, slowed traffic and made us fifteen minutes late for our appointment. Beau hated tardy clients. He stood silently and looked openly upset—probably because we were late or maybe it was due to Dad's passing. Hopefully it wasn't something else.

Dylan tried to lighten Beau's mood as he held out his hand to shake. "Sooo much water out there Beau." Drips fell from Dylan's Cub cap. Beau stood silently and only glared at us, ignored Dylan's hand and simply pointed to the chairs that he expected us to occupy. When we entered, we noticed Alice as she sat alone in the darkness against the wall.

"Alice, wouldya like to join us at the big boy table?" I said with a large scoop of smarmy.

Alice barely looked my way as she hissed, "No thanksss."

"A modicum of civility. This is a legal proceeding after all," Beau curtly demanded. Beau sat, shuffled some papers, cleaned his glasses and slowly sipped on his glass of water. He eventually began, "I can see that the required parties are all present for the reading of the Last Will and Testament of Frank Strong." He exhaled deeply and opened the only envelope on the table. He removed a thin document that I assumed was Dad's will. Beau adjusted his glasses again and began, "I, Frank Strong, being of sound mind and body do hereby bequeath my entire estate to my loving wife, Alice."

Beau stopped and silently reread the paper. He turned the page over to show Dylan and I that there was no more as he stared at us and said, "I don't have anything else."

I reached across the table and grabbed the paper from Beau's hand. "That can't be the real will," I demanded. "On his deathbed, Dad swore to Dylan and me that we would get the business. He said he left everything to us. It had to be true."

Dylan roared, "This is bullshit. We can prove this is a load of crap."

Alice was no longer amused or surprised by the proceedings as she strolled in front of us and looked down her nose while she made a mocking sad-face frown. She leaned forward and put her fists on the table as she sarcastically spewed, "You get nothing."

Alice moved even closer so that her face was inches from ours as she added, "Do you remember when I told you that I'd get it all?" A nasty sneer grew on her lips that looked like the secretive smile of a serial killer. "Well, you little shits, today is the day!"

Alice joyfully beamed as she sauntered over to Beau. She actually hummed to herself as she signed on the lines indicated, initialed in all the appropriate places and made the will final and unquestionably official.

As soon as she walked out of the conference room, I immediately ripped into Beau, "What the hell just happened? You were Dad's friend not just his attorney for thirty-plus years. You just let her walk in this office and steal our business without doing a damn thing? How the hell could you let this happen?"

"I had nothing to do with any of that, hand to God, Rick. All I can tell you is that your old man went around me. I assumed that your dad and Alice decided to alter something personal, just alter. That's what I thought two days ago when I got a package delivered from some hot shot attorney outta Florida. It had an envelope inside that said "Revised Last Will and Testament of Frank Strong." That's what happened, that's all that happened." Beau sounded more upset with me than I was with him.

I refocused and brought my attitude back to reasonable and asked, "How could this have happened, Beau? Dad wasn't in his right mind. There's got to be laws that protect people who are demented and at risk. This can't be legal."

"I'm not sure. Boys, I'm sorry. I don't know enough about Florida law," Beau confessed. "You need someone from there. I'm sorry, but it may all be legal."

"So Alice gets away with this, Beau?" Dylan seethed.

"Until you can overturn the document in court and prove it was done under duress or circumstances out of Frank's control... I guess she does." Beau shrank a little in his chair as Dylan and I marched out of his office.

"What the hell happened in there brother?" screamed a livid Dylan. "If I'm not mistaken, we just got screwed!"

"Damn right, we did!" I furiously replied. "How the hell did this shit happen without us knowing?" I fumed as we stood and waited for the elevator to arrive. After what seemed like an eternity, we took the stairs.

"This is far from over. Round one, that's all," I spouted for my own benefit. My indignation grew with each step we took down. "And you know what the really crappy part is... we can't prove a word of Dad's deathbed declaration. No one heard him say a damn thing." My thoughts quickly moved past what should have been to what would be. I forcefully stated, "Whatever it takes D, we've gotta do something. That asshat Wanton must pay for screwin' with us."

"Then, let's do it. These thieves aren't untouchable," Dylan sharply added.

I felt a surge of confidence race through me as my mind jumped into overdrive. This felt to me like the time we decided to illegally parasail off the Martin skyscraper downtown. We wouldn't be stopped then and absolutely nothing would stop us now.

By the time we reached the lobby I knew what had to be done. I grabbed Dylan by the shoulders and said, "It's time we bring the fight to them and stop these bastards. I say we go after them and take back everything those assholes stole." I stopped long enough to scan the lobby to make sure no one could possibly overhear as I whispered, "And I want this fight to get really nasty... for dad! You in?"

"Abso-friggin'-lutely!"

# chapter **19**

"I'M TELLIN' YOU UP front, if you wake my little man, I'll hurt you bad." Mary warned as she poured herself a second cup of coffee. "Don't you two sleep? I still don't understand why we have to meet at my house. Have you boys forgotten that we have a lovely conference room right in the office?" She said with a hint of upset. Mary obviously wasn't interested in entertaining this early.

"The office is bugged, Mary. When Ezra paid us a little visit, his guy Fix planted a listening device. We found one, but there may be more," Dylan said.

"Sorry, Mary," I apologized. "We know it's the weekend and your day to sleep in, but the bank gave us a tough deadline and we have so much to accomplish. Your apartment was nearby and the only location we could both agree was secure. Was it alright that we invaded your home?"

Still half asleep Mary nodded her answer while she sipped from her 'World's Best Mom' mug. "Sure, Rick, but like I said, we gotta be quiet. And, next time... I'll expect a call in advance." She laid her head down on the kitchen table and closed her eyes.

"Alright then, let's get into this," I said while I set up my white board. I grabbed my squeaky pen and began. "We already knew that Alice was responsible for the alterations of the will. She undoubtably manipulated Dad into signing under duress. After that, Alice colluded with Ezra to take our company and ripped off Loyalty at the same time." I put my marker down and spoke directly to Dylan and Mary when I said, "Looks to me like we have two problems here. How about we break these co-conspirators apart and attack them individually? Divide and conquer, right?" I looked at Dylan as he started to spin a quarter on the table—a habit he picked up in college when he needed to focus his thoughts. "Got any ideas, D?" I asked loudly enough to break his concentration.

"Yeah, I have a thought. How about we take 'em out back and I'll rip 'em a new one," he said with a smile, as he continued to concentrate on his quarter.

"Trying to be serious here." I said as I pounded on the table and made the quarter fall. "Do you have any ideas that we could actually use?"

"Yeah, I've got a thought Rick. Remember our friend from military school? Thomas Rubin? I saw that he was recently named assistant state's attorney in Dade County, Florida. And if I'm not mistaken, Florida is the state Alice's little brother does business." Dylan finished with a snide look at me as he picked up his quarter and spun it.

"Yeah, Thomas. I've kept in touch, a little. But you're right, D, he might be the perfect guy. Finally a good idea!" I laughed. Dylan didn't.

"Since you are so close, call the man," instructed a peeved Dylan.

"When we get done here, I'll call." I pointed at the second half of my white board and said, "Now what about Ezra?"

Mary looked up at the sound of his name and with blurry eyes said, "That guy deserves a special place in hell for screwing with us."

"Damn Mary, remind me not to wake you early ever again," Dylan lightly kidded.

"Say, D, I just had a thought." I felt an idea brewing. "We already know most people don't pay close enough attention to detail. What if we can get Ezra to believe that he was only fighting one of us..."

Mary and Dylan's ears perked up as they listened to my idea as it began to crystallize and unfold. I started spit-balling thoughts. "To pull this off, we need to do something he'd never expect, something so extreme, that looks so real, that he has to believe it happened... without question. What I'm thinkin' about is a little foolish and a lot dangerous."

"Sounds crazy. I'm in," said Dylan.

"Give it a minute, D. What's just popped into my head might be way too crazy. It's light years beyond any prank we've ever done."

"Great," Dylan replied. "I'm still in."

"Right now the finished idea isn't there, but let me tell ya what I've got so far." I closed my eyes, as I envisioned the beginnings of a plan. "I'm thinking we create some kind of big monstrous event that would make Ezra absolutely certain we were unable to fight back. Ezra must be convinced that we're finished and he's won." The plan started to crystalize in greater detail. "And Fix needs to watch or participate in this 'accident' or even better, hurt one of us and report back. With something this important Ezra would only believe it from Fix himself. Whatever we do, we'll really need to sell it."

"Did you say... Sell It? That's my department, Rick," chimed Dylan as he stood and statued himself into his best superhero stance. He grinned as he said, "If it means that I get a chance to tangle with Fixie, I am so in."

"Sit down, Super D, and think this through. It's dangerous," Mary huffed as she took another gulp from her coffee cup.

"Mary," I reached out, took her hand, "You have a family and this could get extremely ugly. Maybe it would be better if you sit this one out."

Mary sat up tall in her seat and spoke directly to me when she said, "You are my family. The both of you are my family and I fully understand the risks here. And I know that whatever happens in this fight, it will determine my future, determine the direction of my life and my son's life. So, I choose to stand next to the people I love and trust. I'll fight at your side no matter the outcome. And God save anyone who tries to mess with us." With fire in her eyes, Mary stated, "I'm in."

Dylan put his hand out in front of us. I put mine on his and Mary placed hers on top. "I fear for anyone who gets in Mary's way," said Dylan. "Here's to the plan."

"The plan," Mary and I repeated.

## chapter 20

I FOUND THOMAS RUBIN'S number and placed the call. I was surprised when he answered his own phone. "Thomas Rubin. How may I help you?" It felt good to hear the reassuring voice of our old friend.

"Hello, Thomas, it's been a long time…"

Cut off mid-sentence, Thomas interjected, "My God, is this Rick Strong? Or is this Dylan? I could never tell your voices apart."

"It's Rick. How are you, Thomas?"

"I'm well! Are you in town? I'd love to show off Miami!" Thomas said. "I'm so glad to hear from you. What's up? You well? How's Dylan?"

I smiled to myself and said, "We're good, thanks. But there is something I need to discuss with you. It's time sensitive. If I caught a flight today, would you be able to wedge me into your schedule?"

"Absolutely, Rick, for you I'm available anytime." Then he wisely asked, "How bad is it?"

"Thomas, things have spun completely out of control. We're in trouble and we need your help."

"I'll always be here for you, Rick."

I booked the first flight to Miami and made it to Thomas' office by late afternoon. His name was newly inscribed at the federal building—Thomas Rubin, Assistant State's Attorney - 12th Floor.

The entire office seemed alive and everyone in the space moved with a purpose. I'm not sure why, but this was exactly what I envisioned when I thought of Thomas' workplace. I introduced myself to Mark, Thomas' executive assistant. He said that Thomas was in a meeting, but that he was told to interrupt once I arrived. Thomas immediately came out from an adjoining office and his smile lit up the room. I smiled broadly as he came over to me. "Rick, it is great to see you." Thomas gave me a hug. "I'm glad you're here. What can I do to assist you, my friend?"

I exhaled and felt a wave of relief wash over me. Just being there with Thomas gave me a new sense of security. He's always made me feel comfortable and at home. "Thomas, I've got a story and a half to tell and it may take a while. Can we sit and talk?" Thomas directed us into his office, handed me a bottle of water and asked me to start at the beginning.

I did what I could and detailed all that had transpired. It took the better part of an hour to unload everything that had happened with Dad, Alice, the business and finally, Ezra. As I related my story to

Thomas, I listened to myself and heard my own words. The more I talked, the more it sounded to me like we were taken in a massive con.

Thomas sat quietly and intently listened. I couldn't tell from his expression what he was thinking or if we even had a case. His lawyerly deadpan was perfect. He had only one question, "Were you or your brother ever informed about these changes to the will?"

"We knew nothing until it was too late."

Thomas nodded. "Interesting. I'll put my best crew on this today and let you know what's going on as soon as possible. No promises. Stay by the phone, it shouldn't take long. Don't worry, Rick, I'm here for you." And just like that we completed our meeting, shook hands and said goodbye.

As I headed back to the airport for my flight back home, I felt better. I wasn't sure if it was Thomas or our discussion, but I was re-energized. Even though Thomas had offered no promises, even reiterated that his efforts may not work out, he gave me hope.

Thomas was a beacon of what was good and right. His words and actions inspired me to fight on. So much so that while I waited for my flight, I called and asked Mary if she would make an appointment for me at Loyalty National Bank. I couldn't help but think that a second conversation might soften their attitude toward us and give us more time.

First thing the following morning I was at the bank, dressed in my best and ready to change some minds. "Rick Strong to see Mr. Rend," I stated to Lily the receptionist. I smiled at her, she smiled back, but I knew it was for Dylan.

Bob Rend came out to greet me. From all appearances, he seemed to be in a good mood. He held out his hand to shake and said, "I hope you've come with good news. We're anxious to hear what you're doing to fix this problem. Let's go have a seat in my office."

"Bob, we haven't fixed the problem yet," I said as I sat and clarified our status.

"That's not good, Rick, not what I had hoped to hear. Our board of directors here remain steadfast with their decision. I assumed that you already knew this and took steps to rectify the problem," Bob stated.

"Bob, today I want to plead our case. We've assembled documentation that clearly indicates that outside influences were responsible for the reuse of our collateral. We've also been diligent toward completion of all required paperwork as you directed."

"That's all fine, Rick, but while we've been sitting here, I checked my computer and saw that the secondary loan is still listed as 'in progress' at Wanton Bank. I expected to see the loan status had changed. But nothing has been done and until we see that the loan at Wanton Bank has been completely stopped, Loyalty will be forced to call in your loan. The entire five million dollars must be returned to us by close of business Thursday or we will assume control of FAS." Bob sat quietly as he awaited my response.

"Bob, I need to tell you everything. Please give me a chance. The information we've compiled will change your mind about what has transpired, I know it will."

Bob took a quick look at his watch and with a nod, he indicated that he'd listen. I began my story, told Bob everything and left out nothing. If he was going to intercede on our behalf, he had to understand the entire situation from our point of view. My presentation was compassionate and I finished with a plea for his assistance. "The people here at Loyalty have been our friends and family forever. Please reconsider your position and tell me that there is something Loyalty can do."

Bob had listened. I could see in his eyes that his attitude had softened some. It was just as I had hoped.

"Rick, when this all started I took it personally because I was your loan officer. I was the one who wrote the loan and pushed it past the board. Let's just say when the bad news came in, I was very upset. Now that I've heard this new information compounded with the death of your dad… I'm starting to think there may be more to this than I first thought. Tell you what, I'll bring your story to the boss to see what he thinks. I can't offer anything, but I'll get back to you later today."

"Thanks, Bob, you know this means the world to everyone at the company. Thanks again." I felt the bank now had a clearer picture of what actually took place.

As I was about to leave the bank, Jeff Kim came out of his office. He gave me a warm best-friend hug. "Hey Rick, I'm real sorry about your dad. He was a good man. It must have been quite a shock to you and Dylan. If there's anything I could do..."

"Jeff, thanks. Right now things are strange, to say the least. Too many things have come at us all at once. And with Wanton Bank's attempt to steal the company...," I said as my words trailed off.

"Wanton Bank? What are those con artists doing?"

"More than you know," I said as I invited Jeff to sit down and have a cup of coffee while I unloaded all my problems. I walked him through the entire Wanton story. He was surprised, but not shocked, when he heard that Alice had colluded with Wanton to defraud us, therefore defrauding Loyalty Bank.

Jeff reached out, and apologized. "Rick I should have known you wouldn't intentionally hurt me, sorry." He thought for a moment and continued, "I can see that you guys have a major problem with Wanton Bank. Let me dig into them for you. You never know, I may be able to uncover something helpful."

"Jeff, no matter what was said, we'll always be buds." I considered his offer and said, "You know, I would appreciate it if you would take a look into Wanton. But if you do, you've got to be careful."

"Hey Rick, you know me... I'm always careful, right?" laughed Jeff.

I was almost out the door when I noticed Bob Rend as he waved papers over his head to get my attention. "Rick! I just finished a conversation with my managing director. Totally unbelievable, I've never seen this before. I think he must have a soft spot for you and Dylan because he just directed me to authorize an additional day extension for FAS. That'll make the deadline Friday, end of day. So…" He stopped and looked around the office. In a low pitched confidence he continued, "Let's call it Monday morning first thing. That should allow ample time. Right?" Bob vigorously shook my hand, this time as a friend. "We believe in you, Rick. Now go out there and make this right."

# chapter 21

I PULLED MY CAR into my office parking space just as my cell went off. I saw that it was a Miami number. "Hey, Thomas. You called with news?" I hoped for some sort of breakthrough.

"I have some things to go over with you, Rick, and it's fascinating stuff. Even this attorney, Lewis Vain, made an impression. My team tried to determine if there ever was an attorney as bad as Lewis Vain." Thomas paused for effect, "There wasn't." He refocused on his message and said, "So, after we studied this case, we determined what Lew did and how he attempted to cover it up. Turned out that the law Alice's little brother manipulated was on the books in Florida, enacted as way to stop unscrupulous con men and thieves from harming vets who returned home from a World War and were considered 'mentally unstable'. Lew twisted the law's original intent and made it conform to their current unethical desires."

Thomas stopped with an audible sigh. "I'm sorry, Rick. What he did was slimy, but it's what the courts call 'legal enough'. For a judge to overturn this, we would need to show substantial evidence that some kind of abuse had taken place. Nothing that I've found in any of the documents indicates that your dad was under any form of duress. Unfortunately, all the signatures were his."

My heart sank. I had hoped Thomas might have been able to resolve our problem. "So… I guess we're back to square one. Thanks for all your help and effort, Thomas. Some things are not meant to be. How can we repay you?"

"Rick, would you let me finish?" Thomas inquired. He waited an overly dramatic beat for effect and restarted, "Lew and his crooked law firm tried, but failed, to hide something extremely pertinent to their case amid a ton of nonsense court-related materials. This is a stupid practice used by crappy attorneys. The document they tried to hide turns out to be the backbone of their competency case and it was the sole legal reason allowing them to make alterations to your dad's will. Rick, I'm referring to the psychological examination. Once we found this document and examined its conclusions, we easily determined that it was a total piece of fiction. It clearly showed that the examination never took place. What I'm trying to tell you, Rick, is that my office has found enough evidence to open an active case file against Alice Strong and Lew Vain. And yours truly will head the investigation and personally pay a visit to Lew and Marge Vain first thing tomorrow morning. Rick, what I've been tryin' to tell you is that we're going to put these people away."

I was surprised, stunned and over-the-edge happy when I yelled into the phone, "Thank you, Thomas!"

Early the next morning the doorbell rang at Lew and Marge's bungalow. It was after nine but Marge was still dressed in her bathrobe as she answered the door. She greeted a smallish well-dressed man holding a brief-case in one hand and his business card in the other. He reached out and handed her his card. "Hello, Mrs. Marge Vain? State's Attorney Thomas Rubin."

"Yes," Marge replied with a touch of fear in her voice. She self-checked and nervously straightened the collar of her robe once she realized that she was not dressed for company. She stood in her doorway and felt unsettled as she eyed Mr. Rubin. She had always secretly worried that Lew's law practice would do something illegal that would come back and bite them someday.

"Mrs. Vain, may I come in? I think you and I have some things that we should discuss."

"I can't imagine what you're talking about," Marge said as she stepped aside and allowed Thomas to enter their home.

Thomas walked directly into their dining room and sat at the table. He placed his briefcase on the floor next to his chair as he turned to Marge and said, "I think you should get dressed, Mrs. Vain. Because, if what I think is going happen actually happens, you and I will be going downtown very soon."

Marge nodded as she shuffled down the hallway to her bedroom. On her way, she grabbed her cell phone and called Lew as soon as she shut the bedroom door. "Lew," she whispered forcefully into the phone. "There's a guy here from the state's attorney's office and I don't know what to do. I'm scared, Lew."

Lew sounded shaken when he asked, "Who? What's this guy's name? What did he say?"

"His card says, Thomas Rubin, Assistant State's Attorney. I'll stall him as long as I can but you've got to hurry home, Lew." Marge sensed something bad was about to happen as she hung up.

Marge took her time dressing and idly milled around her bedroom to waste as much time as possible. She kept looking at the clock and wondered why Lew was taking so damn long to get home. He knew she needed his help. Thomas sensed that she was stalling and began to lose his patience. He eventually called out to her, "If you are purposefully avoiding my questioning, I will make a call and ask the police for their assistance to bring you downtown in handcuffs for a more formal investigation. Your choice, Marge."

"Be there in a minute," Marge called back. She joined Thomas in the dining room and timidly asked, "So what's this all about, Mr. Rubin? I really don't know anything at all about my husband's business."

A silent Thomas leered across the table and studied his prey. From what he saw, he was confident their discussion would unearth the truth. He turned on his recorder and began. "Marge, may I call you Marge?" She nodded her approval. Thomas slid his chair closer as he forged ahead. "Let me tell you what I already know. I already know you're involved. I know Alice and Lew colluded to screw the Strong brothers out of their inheritance." He paused for effect, then quickly renewed his attack. "What I'm attempting to ascertain, with our little informal talk this morning, was just how deeply you were involved with this plot to defraud." He stopped again. "Marge, unless you can clarify these allegations, there is a better than average chance that you will go to prison."

Thomas knew that he had openly lied to her about what he could prove. He waited and watched for her to show signs of weakness. "Well, Marge, are you about ready to tell me the truth?"

He noticed her upper lip had started to sweat. "If this conversation ends without me knowing all the details of what actually transpired, I will make damn sure you never see the sun again. Are we crystal clear, Mrs. Vain?" Thomas stared down at a scared and shaken Marge and waited for her response.

It didn't take long. Marge's eyes filled with tears as she broke down and cried. She momentarily left the dining room and brought back a box of tissue. She blew her nose and wiped her tears as she began her confession to Thomas. "It was all Alice," she loudly sobbed. "She forced us to do everything." Marge's hysterics ebbed momentarily as she peeked over her tissue at Thomas for his reaction after her first attempt at lying. She instantly saw that Thomas saw through her lie and that he seemed to be losing his patience. Marge reconsidered her approach and restarted, "Lew only did what she told him to do." She felt Thomas' hard gaze as it burned right through her—she began to uncontrollably sob. Then, like a dam had just burst, the details of the plot flowed from her like an untamed torrent of information. "Alice came to us over a year ago and forced Lew to find a way to change Frank's will. It was Alice who wanted to get more. I swear, Lew only did what she made him do. I had nothing to do with this... It was all Alice and Lew."

Thomas sat back and listened to Marge's disclosures. He didn't expect a full confession from her without a much greater effort and was surprised, yet grateful, that Marge had made his job simpler. He had heard of confessions like this on TV crime dramas, but in the real world no one had ever given it up this easily—at least no one he had ever questioned. It wasn't long until she had filled his recorder with the complete history of their nasty conspiracy.

Just as she finished and told Thomas everything, Lew barged through the front door. His heart dropped when he saw his teary-eyed wife as she sat uncomfortably with a smiling state's attorney.

"Hello Lew," beamed Thomas as he patted on the chair next to his. "Come on in and take a seat, make yourself comfy and try to relax."

That was the moment Lew realized that his life had ended. He prayed Marge wouldn't go down with him.

# chapter **22**

"YO, RICK," THOMAS CHIMED over the phone, now back in his own office. "Remember that little concern that we discussed about your dad's will? Well, worry no more, my friend. Florida's best newest assistant state's attorney is going to make that entire problem disappear. Or more precisely, my office took the first steps to make it go away."

He waited for me to realize what he had just said. "Did ya hear me Rick?"

"Is this real?" I said, not expecting anything this incredible.

"It was easy," Thomas said. "All I had to do was apply some extreme Rubin pressure." He stopped and I knew he was smiling. "Then they were helpless, I left them with no way out. Lew and Marge both caved and gave me everything I wanted. My office has already prepared a case against Alice and Lew. Once a judge sees this, I'm sure they'll be spending a long time in matched

8 x 10 cells, sporting prison orange jumpsuits. And, to make this call just a little sweeter, I wanted to give you a heads up that the Chicago PD has sent a couple officers to arrest and detain Alice for her arraignment."

"You did all this?" I was surprised and elated at the same time. "What does this mean exactly? How will this effect... everything?"

"As soon as Alice is in custody, I'll petition the court to vacate the last will and make the prior document the real deal," Thomas happily informed. "On the fun side... I was thinkin'... since you guys are soooo close to Alice, you may want to take this opportunity and say goodbye. I was told that she'll be transported to the Fifth Street lockup and held there overnight. She should arrive there around six."

"Thomas, you are brilliant!" I yelled into the phone. "Thank you so much from both of us, from all of us!" I'm sure he felt my exuberance and relief over the phone as I praised our newest best friend. "I'm amazed you did this so fast. We're in your debt forever. Anything, anything you want, my first kid will be named Thomas, anything." My excitement bubbled over.

"Rick, are you kidding me? I'll always be in your debt. Back at the Academy, I couldn't ask for your help. But you two were there for me and righted the wrong of Marco. You stood up for me when I couldn't do it for myself. My family just wanted money from the whole ordeal, but as far as I'm concerned, it was you and Dylan who saved me. I love you both like brothers." Thomas told me he would stay close and simply said goodby.

I couldn't wait to tell Dylan and Mary. I felt over the top but I attempted to contain my excitement when I asked in the dullest voice I could muster, "Do either of you want to go say goodbye to Alice?" I waited until I heard Dylan moan.

"What's this about, Rick?" Mary asked.

"Just about a minute ago, I got a call from our new best friend and attorney, Thomas Rubin. He told me that Lew gave up Alice and that they will both face charges. He also mentioned that the CPD had sent officers to arrest Alice, as we speak. Said she'd arrive at the Fifth Street lockup sometime around six tonight, probably in handcuffs. I think we should all go and wave bye bye to the bitch. Whatchathink?"

Dylan whooped, "Brother, are you kidding me? Oh yeah, Thomas did it! I want to kiss him on the lips cuz I know I'm in love. I'm gonna scoop up Mary and we'll be there pronto. Only got one stop on the way, bro. That's to buy the largest bottle of scotch I can find." I heard Dylan let out a primal scream as he hung up.

Now take a picture of this: It was just a little before six, Dylan, Mary and I were seated in my comfy Cub lawn chairs on the sidewalk just outside the Fifth Street lockup. We had already downed a couple three shots in anticipation of the event and felt totally relaxed as we waited for Alice in chains. At about six, a squad car rolled up into a space directly in front of us. A handcuffed Alice exited the car and immediately saw the three soused amigos as we held up shots of scotch and toasted her demise.

"Bon Voyage, Bee-och," Dylan said as he jumped up and started to do the wave, I quickly followed, then Mary. We repeated and improved our timing with each reoccurring set as we waved goodbye.

"This ain't over, you shits," an enraged Alice spewed. "The charges will never stick."

I couldn't help it—I had to hold my ribs because they ached from laughing. We did another quick shot and started to sing the refrain from an old song by Steam. "Na na na na, na na na na, hey hey hey, good-bye." The three of us swung our arms over our heads, repeated and repeated again that memorable chorus until Alice was well out of sight. Even the cops laughed out loud. Man, that was too much fun.

Then, without thinking, all three of us joined voices and screamed loud enough so she clearly heard, "Friggin' Alice."

It was a short cab ride for los tres amigos as we stumbled into the office completely wasted. We believed it was our duty to do our best to finish off the bottle of scotch. "Let's toast Thomas," I slurred.

Dylan grabbed the office phone, put it on speaker and called our new hero Thomas. "Thomas Rubin," he politely answered.

"Thomas," the three of us screamed more or less in unison. "You are the best lawyer in the entire civilized world. Correct that, the universe."

Thomas was slow to respond as he somberly replied, "Guys, thanks, but I've got some bad news." He paused and we sensed that there was something new to be worried about. "I'm sorry, but no one saw this coming."

He stopped again and seemed to be collecting his thoughts when he finally said, "When Alice got to the Fifth, she was admitted and placed into a holding cell. A short time later, she instigated a verbal confrontation with another woman over the seating arrangements in the cell. After Alice called her a 'dyke', the other woman was so enraged that she brandished a knife and repeatedly stabbed Alice in the face and neck. Guys, Alice died on the way to the hospital."

# chapter **23**

THE NEXT MORNING I woke at my desk. The entire side of my face hurt because I think I slept on a pencil. I coughed hard and woke Mary who was still asleep on my couch. I had no idea she crashed here last night. She sat up, stretched and yawned out loud as she rubbed her eyes. She slowly got up only to immediately sit down in the chair in front of my desk.

I watched her as she twisted and turned in a vain attempt to get comfortable. I softly asked, "Did we actually finish that bottle?" I pressed my fingers to my aching temples. I felt the weight of each spoken word as they reverberated and collided inside my skull. "It feels like we finished the bottle."

"I don't know. I stopped at the fourth or fifth toast to Thomas and closed my eyes for a sec," Mary recounted as she deeply yawned again. "Call Dylan. Get him to bring a large bottle of aspirin."

"Got your aspirins right here, Mary," said a chipper Dylan as he marched into my office. "If you need more of them, I've replenished our supply in the bathroom cabinet. Isn't everyone having a beautiful morning?"

Dylan strutted around the office like a satisfied rooster and looked totally refreshed. He must have grabbed a shower because he emanated the scent of an expensive musk. "Hey guys, let's wake up here. Yesterday was Alice day. Today, we scrape another equally disgusting piece of crap off the bottom of our other shoe." Dylan began to snap his fingers as fast as he could. "Come on guys, let's go." Then he turned to me and pressed an already known point, "Rick, I told you last night not to try to drink that entire bottle of scotch or you'd pay. Remember last time you had too much of a good thing?"

"It's not a hangover. I think I slept on a pencil," I said as I stood and stretched. "Did you sleep at all?" I asked as I moved my head from side to side and listened to it emit unnatural sounds. Each vertebrae snapped, then crackled and finally popped as I moaned, "How about we let my head catch up to the morning, Dylan. Can't you see Mary and I aren't even awake yet?"

"Leave me out of this," barked Mary the Grouch. "I'll have nothing to do about anything for either of you this early. The sitter gave me 'til noon, so I'm sleepin' in. Anyhow, after last night's celebration and how my head feels right now, I just want to go back to dreaming about ice cream with rainbow sprinkles."

My office phone rang and its trill was particularly harsh this morning. "Good day, Rick Strong here." I sounded as feeble as I felt.

"Rick, Jeff Kim here. Got a sec?"

"Sure, should I put you on speaker?"

"Probably not. I've found some detailed information about Wanton Bank. This shouldn't be heard by unwanted listeners," Jeff warned, knowing about the listening device in my office.

"Go ahead, just tell me what you need, Mr. Grace," I said for the sake of Ezra's bug. I motioned for both Dylan and Mary to move closer.

Jeff began. "I was so right to look into Wanton Bank. Dude, they're barely a bank. Over the last two years, their charter has been revoked three times. Each time, something miraculous occurs and the bank is allowed back in business. My connection at the regulatory commission told me that the feds had already instigated disciplinary action to shut the bank down. This sounds imminent, Rick. There's more. Ezra was personally under investigation by the feds for bank fraud and money laundering. From what I've ascertained, he's got the two of you in his crosshairs. He wants your business so you've got to be very careful."

I scribbled notes of the entire conversation for Dylan and Mary. It was not a surprise to either of them that Ezra had decided to come after us.

I cryptically answered Jeff, "Well, the brake pads you've indicated will certainly work out just right for your needs Mr. Grace." I kept up with our ruse for the trolls at the other end of the microphone. "I'm sure we can take care of things from here. I don't want you to take any more of your time with this. I know you understand. Thanks."

"Sure, Rick, I understand what you're sayin'. So you know, I prepared full documentation about everything. I need to take one more look at Wanton tonight. I saw something in a ledger I want to check out. Talk later." Jeff hung up.

All of us stood around my desk and I thought about what Jeff had said. I quickly jotted down a note as I stared directly at Dylan. "No heroics, we stick to the plan, right?" I fixed my gaze on Dylan and waited for his reply.

"Yeah, sure, I'll stick to the plan," Dylan wrote as he rolled his eyes. He took out a bigger sheet and wrote in large letters, "But Mr. Fix gets special attention." Dylan smiled at me and turned to Mary while he held up a hand and waited for a high five. Mary ignored him.

I positioned myself close to Dylan as I firmly but quietly stated, "These guys will kill you, bury you in a corn field and get pleasure from it. If we're going after Ezra, you've got to keep your head in the game, Dylan. Because if you screw this up, even a little, we're both dead. Together we win, alone we don't. Stick to the plan, Dylan," I finished sternly. "No damn games."

My cell rang and we both jumped. I answered, "Hello, Rick here."

"Hey Rick, it's Bob Rend from Loyalty. I've got some good news about the product shipment."

"Good news? I always welcome that. Let me put you on speaker. Mary and Dylan are here."

"Hey Mary, Dylan. Good to talk to you all. I just wanted to let you know that I had a personal conversation with a dispatcher from the transport company that's moving your product. She said it has left the dock and should arrive at your facility in just over a week, barring any difficulties. The only thing that remains for you to do is get all that paperwork to me like you promised. And just so you know, we're all pulling for you over here."

"You're the best Bob," was my response. "We won't let you down."

We quietly cheered this news. The balance of power had finally started to shift our way. Sometime soon, we might be able to get our lives back. We kept that thought in check because we clearly understood that good fortune and luck would only take us so far.

After what we heard from Bob, we knew the time was right to go on the offensive. Not a balls out offensive, more like a 'mess with Ezra's head' kind of offensive. We wanted Ezra's attention to be on anything but us. The time was right for some reverse psychological warfare.

I wrote a quick note to Mary and Dylan: Follow My Lead.

"Dylan," I said. "This might be something important, check this out." I paused for effect. "I got an email from my cop friend today. He leaked some pretty damaging information about Wanton Bank. Looks like the feds are getting involved."

Mary tried to sound totally natural when she asked, "Does the email say that there will be a raid?" Dylan and I stopped and looked directly at Mary. I mouthed "A raid?"

Dylan jumped into the conversation. "I got that same email, Rick. Did you open the attachment?" Dylan looked my way, bounced his eyebrows and grinned. "Looks like whatever the feds had in mind, it's going to be happening soon. The judge heard their petition and gave the feds a search warrant which should be served as early as this afternoon." Dylan smiled and put his hands up in one of those 'is that good?' gestures.

We all fought off urges to laugh. "That will screw with Ezra's head," I said to myself. It was tactically a good move to mess with Ezra. At the same time, we knew his history and it was clear that he would fight like a caged animal if he ever felt trapped.

I scribbled another note: Get some rest. Tomorrow we give Ezra a real bad day.

# chapter 24

DYLAN AND I MET in his office early the next morning. We didn't talk much other than to greet one another as we came in. I thought it was nerves. Dylan said it was because he was hungry.

"How about we grab some greasy eggs and bacon somewhere before we deal with Ezzie and his pet, Mr. Fix," Dylan said, a bit too enthusiastically.

"All right, we could visit Eddie's E-licious Eggs. I know you like the waitress there." I waited for his usual response.

He didn't disappoint. "Oh, oh my sweet Olivia Overtoss. That woman has got the cutest pair of eggs that ever went over easy." Dylan closed his eyes, pointed to the sky as he undoubtedly made a nasty wish. He smiled broadly and said, "I'm ready to get some."

Eddie's is one of those diner dives made from a converted railroad car. Inside was a long narrow counter in front of the grill and four tiny booths barely large enough for each to seat four. It wasn't spacious and the food was barely edible but Olivia worked there. Today, she met us at the door, handed me the menu and whispered to Dylan that she was serving up eggs with something special on the side. Dylan gave her a devilish grin and walked to his favorite booth. Olivia followed him there and gave him his personal appetizer—a big kiss on the cheek. As Dylan went for an extra sweet serving from Olivia, I ordered my breakfast. Hold the syrup.

I tapped loudly on the table to unlock Dylan's eyes from Olivia's ass as she sashayed off. "Let's go over our objectives for the meeting this morning. Seriously, Dylan, head in the game, remember? Tell me what we already know?"

Dylan listed, "Ezra knows Alice is dead and her idiot brother is under arrest and ready to turn on him in a heartbeat. We let him hear that FAS Inc.'s product will arrive from Seattle soon. Then there was our bull-shit conversation about the feds and he probably thinks they are ready to close in on him and his business," Dylan listed. "So, what's next?"

"We complicate his life, add a touch of stress and axe the bogus business agreement he thought he had with Alice. And as always, we'll find a way to leave him with our lovely lasting impression. How does that sound to you?"

"Sweet!"

We finished our meal and I paid the bill while Dylan got a little to go from Olivia. We started for the door when my cell rang. It was Jeff.

"Jeff, what's going on?" I thought it was odd that he called, because we had agreed that he was not going to pursue this.

"I'm in my car on my way to you. I found new information late last night that you've got to hear about right now. But not on the phone. I'm also a little worried that Wanton may have found out I hacked his computer. Not good." Jeff sounded out of breath. "Jesus Christ, I just had to swerve to avoid an oncoming car! What the hell? Hold on, Rick. I got some jerk weed tailgating me. What does this idiot want and why the hell is he flashing his bright lights? He's practically up my rear!"

Then click, the phone went dead. I held the phone out and said to Dylan, "Lost the connection."

What we later learned… Jeff never saw and couldn't possibly have evaded was the heavily loaded garbage truck that violently slammed into his driver's side door. The collision was so intense that his car was shoved entirely off the road across the sidewalk and partially into a pizza parlor on the corner. Once the truck finally came to a stop, it sat atop Jeff's crushed car hood and idled. Eventually, air brakes released, gears ground and the truck slowly backed off. Jeff was pinned in his vehicle, but alive. The truck lurched forward and crashed again into the mangled pile of steel as it attempted to completely obliterate its driver. In the distance sirens wailed as the truck mercifully backed onto the street. Its satisfied driver threw his rig into gear and slowly drove away.

I had no idea what had just happened to our best friend.

Our drive downtown was unusually low on traffic, which allowed us time to arrive at Ezra's office just after ten. Our attitude worsened after we got on the excessively slow elevator that crept painfully from floor to floor. What made it worse was the selection of repulsive music that was played. When we finally got to the seventh floor, Mr. Fix wasn't atop his usual perch. We walked past the sleepy secretary and strolled silently into Ezra's office. Fix nudged Ezra to make him aware we were in the room. I'm not sure why, but they seemed to have expected us. Fix stepped from behind Ezra's desk and circled toward Dylan. Ezra stayed behind his desk and stood awkwardly. I moved to his right side and put him within my range. Cozy.

"What the hell are you bastards doing in my office? Shouldn't you be at home filling out paperwork for the bank? I heard you've only got a couple more days to save the company," Wanton snickered to himself. "I'm not canceling the loan—so we have nothing to discuss."

I moved to a more advantageous position closer to Ezra in case he got upset with my news and attempted to lash out. "Ezra, as you may already know, your buddy and close business associate, Alice, won't be joining us today, or any day for that matter—cuz she's being permanently detained by Satan. So we've stopped by to officially terminate the bullshit agreement you struck with her to steal our company. It ain't gonna happen,

Ezzie." I stepped nearer to him and said as coldly as I could, "Your services are no longer needed or wanted. Don't ever bother us again."

"Or else what, punk? Is that supposed to scare me?" Ezra replied. He had been threatened by many men and knew how to give it back. "We're not done here, son. The contract is signed, sealed and you both are still mine. Now, get the hell out of my office and next time, only come when I whistle for you," Ezra fumed. "Mr. Fix, show them out."

Mr. Fix took a step toward Dylan, his gun already out of its holster. "How fast are you now, little man?" asked Fix of Dylan. "How about you show me how fast you think you are right now."

Dylan and Fix locked onto each other's moves. Dylan stayed with his aggressive style and poked the dog as he said, "Looks like you're afraid, Fixie? I heard you got slow when you were in prison and that you still cry yourself to sleep at night." Dylan assumed if he chided Fix it would keep him off guard.

Ezra sneered and lit up a cigarette. He took a deep drag and blew the stench directly at me. There was a limit of what I'd take from this creep. Without warning, I reached out and grabbed the cigarette from Ezra's mouth and purposefully extinguished it on his wooden desktop. He was totally shocked. As I did that, Dylan moved inside Fix to counter his movements. Fix knew he was boxed into a corner so he shifted his position and raised his gun. As soon as he did, Dylan kicked hard and fast. The kick stunned Fix's gun hand and he lost control. The gun flew into the air, landed on the floor and spun away from both men. I stood and watched Dylan as he landed a hard right when, without warning, a single gunshot blast erupted behind me. I spun around and saw Ezra holding the gun over his head as plaster fell from the ceiling. He quickly lowered the weapon and trained it on me.

The expression on his face was cold and told me everything. "Get out of my office, or I shoot you where you stand," Ezra threatened. "You Strong boys are such morons! You have no idea what's going on right under your collective noses. I'll tell you this once and only once... Screw with me and you'll pay." He waved the gun back and forth from me to Dylan. "You both think you're so smart. So did your pal Jeff Kim when he hacked into my computer last night. He thought he was good, but my IT guy was better. Now he's paid the price. This is your last warning, cretins—or more people that you care about will suffer."

Ezra kept the gun pointed at us as we slowly exited past his door and out of his office. When we got to the elevator, I looked at Dylan. "What did he mean when he said Jeff paid the price?" I asked, not expecting him to answer.

Once we got outside onto the sidewalk, I punched in Jeff's number on my cell. The call went straight to voice mail. I hung up and tried his office number. The bank receptionist, Lily, answered his extension as she cried. "Jeff was in a terrible car accident. A truck t-boned him into a building while he was on his way to your office. It took the jaws of life to get him out of his mangled Subaru. He's barely alive in the ICU."

Dylan and I raced to the hospital and ran to the ICU. The nurse at the desk remembered us. Like Dad's hospital room, there were so many wires, so many sounds that binged and beeped. I started thinking about losing Dad, but then I saw Jeff. He body was casted from head to toe. We were told that both of his legs and an arm had multiple fractures, three ribs were broken and he had a punctured lung. The facial lacerations that covered most of his left side were stitched and left him six shades of purple. He moaned as he opened his right eye and saw us.

I gently put my hand on his and softly said, "We're here, Jeff. We're here for ya, man. Tell us what happened."

"It's Wanton, Rick. He must of hired..." Jeff fought back the wave of pain as he coughed, winced and fell back onto his pillow.

"Who, Jeff? Who did Wanton hire?"

Jeff inhaled and grit his teeth in pain as he warned, "Assassins, Rick. I saw details on Wanton's computer that he hired assassins!" Jeff looked deep into my eyes to make sure I understood his warning before his eyes closed and he fell unconscious.

Nurse Betty stood and held the door. "Jeff needs his rest. You two should go down the hall and try to relax.

If something happens, I'll let you know. It's going to be a long night." Her voice sounded convincing, almost reassuring, but we still worried.

chapter **25**

NURSE A. BETTY WAS the ICU superstar who was assigned to Jeff for the night. We found out that the 'A' in her name stood for Apple. She hated the name. A five year veteran of ICU, Nurse Betty developed a reputation for being the first person into the room whenever trouble struck. Jeff's ER physician specifically chose her to watch over Jeff for the next eight hours due to the high probability that he would code. Nurse Betty constantly monitored Jeff and I monitored her. If anything went south with him, she would be the first to jump. She was determined not to let him down and made me believe that Jeff would find his way back. Her compassion for our friend reminded me of our mom. I waited nearby just in case there was a code blue.

His first code was within twenty minutes, and then there were two more. Dylan couldn't relax and frustratedly paced the floors. His friend was in pain and there was nothing he could do. He finally stopped, sadly looked at me and said, "Damn it, Rick. Jeff was doing us a favor. He got crushed because of us. It's all our fault." Dylan felt his pain.

Ezra wanted us to feel Jeff's pain.

We needed to break the tension so I suggested we go down to the cafeteria for some coffee when Jeff coded once again. Nurse Betty flew to his side. From the waiting area, we heard her scream, "Come back! Jeff! You are not dying tonight!" New alarms sounded. More doctors and nurses ran into his room. "Damn it, Jeff," yelled a now angry Nurse Betty. "Don't you ever scare me like that again," she said quieter now. Dylan and I were standing in the hallway as she came out of his room. She wiped her forehead as she walked over to us and said, "That man is tough. If he stays with us for the next few hours... I think he may just make it." Dylan and I exhaled simultaneously. We hadn't realized that we'd both been holding our breath.

Time crawled, only to be jump-started several times through the night by Nurse Betty who miraculously fought back death. We felt useless, just like when Dad was in the hospital. We begged for information, but Nurse Betty wouldn't or probably couldn't say how Jeff was doing and we were getting restless. Restless enough to count the exact number of ceiling tiles between the waiting room and Jeff's room. It was148. I'm certain, I counted twice.

My cell vibrated. I checked the number and it wasn't one I knew so I let it go to voicemail. A minute later it annoyingly chimed to let me know someone had left a message. I put it on speaker.

"Hello, Rick, I've received some disconcerting news that requires your immediate attention. When time permits, call." The deep voice was unmistakable. It was Gatlin Brown. We hadn't heard from Gat for years—not since our days together at the can plant.

I immediately called him back. "Gat, it has been a long time. How is everyone in your family?"

"All has gone well in my world," he said. "But I felt compelled to reach out to you and your brother after I received details of something imminent from a trusted member of my circle." Gat measured his words as though he were about to reveal something secretive. "Turns out some banker dude has initiated a contract for the elimination of two young marks. Turns out these marks are twins." Gat paused as we absorbed the news. "I thought it best we have a private conversation before this upcoming event gets beyond my abilities to manipulate."

As if we didn't have enough problems. I closed my eyes as I thought about Jeff, Dylan and all that needed to be done and said, "Gat, I'm on my way."

I pocketed my cell and turned to Dylan. "D, I'll go see Gat and get this new crap ironed out. You stay here and keep an eye on Jeff. If anything changes...."

Dylan waved me off and said, "Sure, Rick. We'll be just fine. Do what ya can and be sure to say hey to Gat for me."

With this new threat and our dear friend to watch over, Dylan and I had to split up. I thought that I was being expedient as I assigned each of us a task. But I had a gut feeling that Dylan planned to bolt as soon as I was out of his sight. I turned back to Dylan who was doing his best to ignore me. "Don't even think about going after that dipshit by yourself, Dylan. You can't win this one alone. Promise me that you'll stay here and wait!"

"Sure, Rick. No worries, I'll wait for ya," he said with zero conviction.

I walked over to Nurse Betty as I looked directly at Dylan and spoke, "Nurse Betty, as soon as I walk out that door, my dumbass brother is planning to leave and try to exact some kinda revenge for Jeff. You and I both know he's just going to get himself hurt. So, for his own safety, is there something that you could do to make sure he doesn't leave?"

"Hold him down, I'll get a shot of something that'll knock him out," she threatened as she stood over him with a no-nonsense gaze.

"Alright, alright, I get it, I'll stay put," Dylan surrendered as he held up both hands.

I felt somewhat sure that he would stay put, especially after Nurse Betty's threat. I left the ICU, plugged in Gat's address into my map app and shot off to see him. I wasn't sure what to expect because it had been more than a decade since we had all worked together. I hadn't kept in touch as much as I wanted. I should have been a better friend.

The only thing that Dylan told me was that Gat had become the right hand man to the newly elected Alderman in his neighborhood. The way Dylan explained the job was that Gat was the one called when things needed to be fixed. Hopefully, they were all legal. From my vantage point, this job was ideal for Gat. He got paid well, did what he does best and had time to pursue his personal agenda.

For as long as I've known Gat, he's talked about the development of a concept that he called 'a circle of friends'—an ever growing cooperative that invites people and businesses to join together to do the things they do best for the benefit of everyone in the neighborhood. He believes whole-heartedly this ideal will create a world where everyone will feel safe and secure.

In one of the many conversations that I had had with Gat back in the day, we discussed the origins of his circle. He totally believed that he was born into it. But I disagreed. As I saw it, responsibility and caring for others was forced upon him at the early age of six. His parents were both employed full-time and as the eldest son, he was put in charge of the well-being of his two younger sisters. Even though his sisters were more than a handful to keep on the straight and narrow, he constantly told others that he loved doing it. Regardless of circumstances that faced their family, Gat made sure his sisters were never hurt, never joined gangs and finished high school with honors.

To verify how much he gave personally to protect them, Gat pulled up his shirt and began counting the scars he had received from knife fights and beatings. He stopped counting at fifteen. He explained that in order to make his family safe, he learned to fight. "I stopped punks from hurting my sisters and sometimes I got knocked down. But you always defend your family! That's most important—No matter what."

After he had finished his second tour in the Marines, the only job locally available was at Rightway. After the can plant failed, Gat was recruited by the Alderman to help him clean up his new district. Gat accepted the job because he felt that working for an Alderman would put him in a position to help elevate others and expand his circle. He wanted everyone to experience the mutual benefits of working for something greater than themselves.

While he worked at the can plant, Gat's circle was comparatively small. It only included the people close to his daily routine—neighbors in his building, friends at work and those whom he saw as beneficial to his causes. Now as the Alderman's right hand, Gat reveled in the increased number of circle members and treasured the addition of their unique talents. He personally worked with everyone who joined the cooperative. They in turn gave back to the community with generous donations of their time, their finances or anything that would elevate others. A major pay-it-forward thing became commonplace within his circle's neighborhood.

As the circle's financial needs grew, Gat used his expansive city-based connections and found ways to assist. He negotiated with local businesses to reduce costs, developed a food and clothing co-op and convinced a venture capital company to fund and open a massive hydroponic vegetable farm in an abandoned factory building. But his ultimate accomplishment was when he persuaded an independent physician's group to open an office to serve his community and simultaneously offer healthcare plans at reduced, more realistic prices. The community loved it, local businesses thrived and the Alderman was praised for his ability to get things done.

Once the neighborhood's capabilities for good expanded, they were equaled by its ability to protect itself against any adversary. From within Gat's circle, designated security officers were selected from those willing to walk a beat. They were well trained and equipped to protect while they patrolled the streets within their district 24/7. Each shift openly shared information with the police and coordinated their efforts. The entire neighborhood became a safe haven and was secured against gangs and outside agitators. People in surrounding neighborhoods knew better than to mess with Gat and his circle. Retribution for hurting any neighborhood member was always swift and extremely harsh. Gat grew to believe that helping others and providing for their protection was now his personal destiny.

The more Gat's world grew for the good, the more cognizant he was of the presence of unlawful individuals who resided in the neighborhood. Though not pleased, Gat allowed this coexistence to continue, but only under his terms. They were simple—No one in his circle would ever be harmed in any way and all the illegal underground information that constantly circulated in his neighborhood would be directed to Gat. He felt this little indiscretion into the dark side was tolerable as long as he was able to keep his finger on the entire pulse of the neighborhood.

Always watchful for opportunities, Gat was made aware of an intriguing offer from a devious and unscrupulous individual, which he decided to accept: it was the contract to eliminate the Strong brothers for Ezra Wanton.

I arrived without delay at the address that I plugged into my phone. The building was a large four story all brick edifice that reminded me of a bank. Some scaffolding was still up from a recently remodeled exterior which now sported a sleek modern design. From what I could tell as I looked around, many buildings in the nearby area were under construction at various stages of completion. I felt that all this was undoubtedly possible because of Gat's new position and his influence in the neighborhood.

I got out of my car and went into the building. The main floor was open, clean and had that new construction smell. I buzzed his apartment, walked into the entryway and took the elevator to the top floor. The doors opened and I saw Gat as he walked out to greet me. He smiled as he gave me a hug. He was physically larger and appeared to be incredibly fit. "It makes my heart warm to see you again, brother," he stated.

We walked from the elevator into his apartment as I admitted, "It's been too long, Gat. I'm sorry I haven't kept in touch. That's all on me. I just sorta let life get in the way of seeing the people I care about."

"No worries, Rick. All that matters is family and you're here now." Gat pointed to the chairs in his living room for us to sit. He strolled around and sat in a seat next to mine. His tone became more somber as he said, "I heard about your dad. Sorry, man. Losing any family member hurts, but losing your dad is heartbreaking."

"Thanks. It was rough and it still hurts." I shifted in my seat and made myself comfortable as I looked closely at my old friend. He had grown more mature but didn't outwardly show any of the signs of age. His body language still exuded confidence and when I looked into his eyes, I could see that he already knew about our problems and understood that they were well beyond our ability to control.

"Looks like we've got something serious to deal with here, Rick," Gat started by stating the obvious.

He stroked his beard and a little grin crossed Gat's lips as he contemplated what to do next. Before he had a chance to say anything, I spoke, "I assume you already know all about our situation and everything that has transpired to date." Gat knowingly nodded and I continued, "I'm also pretty certain that Ezra was the one who put out the contract." Again Gat nodded. "Then, what are we to do?"

Gat smiled once more and made a 'wait a minute' indication with his index finger as he poured us each a glass of wine and said, "I'm not sure how to break this to you, Rick, but I'm the individual who accepted Wanton's contract and unfortunately... I'll be forced to kill you and Dylan."

As his words echoed in my head, my facial expression must have been somewhere between scared shitless and hilariously stupefied. Because as soon as Gat finished pouring, he looked at my face and started into the deepest most gut-busting laughter I've heard from anyone. "I accepted the contract to save your silly white asses, you fool," he bellowed.

I felt like a fool. For what seemed like an eternity, Gat continued his laughter until it finally began to ebb. I sat and quietly waited. But as soon as he looked at me again, it started all over. "Ohhhh, thanks, man, can't remember when I had a laugh like this." Over the next five minutes, he continued to intermittently laugh out loud at my expense.

After Gat's funny bone had been fully appeased, we went through the details of what I believed would be a good plan to stop our enemy. Gat listened and considered, then finally said, "Nice plan, I like what's been done so far. But now that my circle has been brought in, we'll be forced to alter a few details to insure its proper outcome." I appreciated there were unseen details that only he knew and that I would never know. We spent some time and discussed the changes to the plan.

"We owe you, Gat."

"No worries really, it's what we do for family. Now, it's time for you to get back to your brother at the hospital because the upcoming commotion is already in motion."

# chapter **26**

"A SHOT AND A score!" Dylan announced to himself.

I found him in a quiet corner of ICU shooting crumpled magazine pages into a now over-filled trash can. "Did ya win?" I asked.

"No," he flatly stated. "What's up with Gat?"

"When it's halftime I'll fill ya in. But before I get into that, there's something you should hear from me." I paused and confessed with my head down. "I made an ass of myself today."

Dylan smiled for the first time since Jeff was hurt and asked, "Whatchado?"

I told him about what happened at Gat's place. I even tried to minimize the embarrassing details, but Dylan laughed out loud at my expense too. Sure hated being the fool twice in one day. Regardless of how I felt, it made my little brother feel better, more relaxed. I heard his stomach growl and realized that we had missed a couple meals. We went down to the cafeteria and had the special of the day—something disgusting covered in gravy. That was a mistake.

On the way back to the ICU waiting area, we ran into a young guy who showed us his badge. "I'm Vinny DeMano, I'm with the Cyber Crimes Division, Mary's cousin. You guys the Strong brothers?"

"It's about time someone from the department showed up," I infuriatedly said. "This was all Ezra Wanton. We know he did this. When are the police going to do something?"

Officer DeMano took the seat next to mine and pulled out his notepad. He read through his notes and reviewed what he already knew. "So let me get this straight... Mary came to my office the other day and asked me about this guy Wanton. She said you two wanted information about this scumbag cuz he was screwin' wit you somehow. Then your buddy Jeff there tries to help you out and wound up gettin' himself crushed by a garbage truck. Is that about right? Anything you boys want to add?" Vinny questioned.

Dylan and I sat quietly.

"Got nothin? Then let me ask you two this—What the hell do you think you're doin' and why are you screwin' with this criminal?"

Vinny eyed us and patiently waited for our response. His actions made me believe he expected information from us that he already knew, something we hadn't given him yet. But he never said anything, he never pressed. Because of Mary, we trusted Vinny and after the conversation I had with Gat, I realized that it was time to involve the police. From our chairs in the waiting room, Dylan and I told Vinny everything. I included all the reworked details of the plan.

Vinny listened and scribbled notes. When we finished he said, "I'm glad you two finally decided to fill me in. You shoulda confided in me sooner. You know that doncha? My guys at cyber already knew about some nasty activity on the dark web. And, we knew it was directly tied to you two jamokes. I don't want to see you boys end up like your buddy Jeff in there. After what that garbage truck did to his Subaru, Jesus Christ... I don't know how the hell he survived that."

"I want five minutes with that truck driver," Dylan stated. "If we find him before you, that son-of-a-bitch gonna hurt real bad." Dylan and I bumped fists.

"Get that crap out of your heads right now. The police will handle this," Vinny officially scolded. "But... if you do happen to catch up to him first..." He inched a little closer and quietly spoke as he said, "Make sure it's an accident." He stood, carefully scanned the waiting area and made certain no one was within ear shot when he finally confided, "You guys should know that we already had a long conversation with Mary about all this. Me and my pals at the station are ready to go anytime. Understand?" Then he added, "Let's get this scumbag." Vinny shook our hands and slowly walked away.

"I like that guy," Dylan said as he watched Vinny move down the hall.

"Mary said he was cool. I like him too." I should have known that friends had been watching out for us.

My cell rang and it was Mary. "Hey Mary, your ears must have been burning. Dylan and I just talked to your cousin Vinny. Cool guy."

Mary didn't respond immediately. When she did, she sounded very nervous. "Rick, I've got a real problem."

By the sound of her voice, I was instantly worried. "What is it, Mary?"

"Mr. Fix is here at my house and he told me he wants Dylan." Mary yelped lightly as Fix took the phone from her and got on the line.

"He gets here in fifteen minutes, or your sweetheart is dead," Fix coldly demanded.

I shot a fearful look to Dylan. The confrontation with Fix was expected, even wanted, but Mary shouldn't be involved. Fix will regret that he did that. Dylan lightly tapped my elbow and said confidently, "I'm good, Rick. This fight is mine and I'm ready. Remember the plan."

I knew he was right, but I still worried. "Watch your six and kick some ass, Dylan. But mostly, be real careful, D."

"Always. And, I love you too, Rick." Dylan flashed a smile, but when I looked into his eyes, I saw that he was afraid.

chapter **27**

THE EVENING HAD BECOME cool and dark as clouds rolled overhead, which made it feel raw. Rain intermittently came down and spat on Dylan's windshield as he drove to Mary's house. The wetness glistened on the roadway and reflected the colors of every streetlight and signal along the drive. Dylan rolled down his window and listened to the soft rustling noise made by the wind as it darted between the leaves and the splashy-hum of his tires on the wet asphalt. He let the sounds and smells of the night surround him to calm his nerves. It felt good.

His drive time should have been short since the traffic was almost non-existent this late at night. But tonight he was overly cautious and purposefully slow. He expected the unexpected and feared the inevitable because he knew he was about to enter a trap. Whatever was to come, he had to be ready. This clash with Fix had to be on Dylan's terms—it was part of the plan.

Dylan pulled up to the curb and parked his car after he located a suitable vantage point that was down the street and across the block from Mary's home. He sat and surveyed the area from his safe spot as he cautiously examined the buildings, the cars in the street and every shadowy space between his car and Mary's door. Tonight, the entire street was unnaturally dark. Heavy clouds hung low overhead and created a misty moonless darkness. The corner street lamps which normally illuminated Mary's entry had been purposefully broken. Mary's front porch, usually bright, was now dark and shrouded in shadows.

Dylan quietly sat and intently listened. He was unable to see his adversaries, but he sensed their presence. There was no sound, no movement. Even the leaves on the trees stood absolutely still as they awaited the upcoming storm. Until something changed, Dylan decided to wait and watch. It wasn't long before he noticed movement coming from the shadows.

Like a ghostly figure in a horror movie, Fix floated out of the blackness and stood silent in front of Mary's house. A low-lying mist swirled around him as he stepped further into view. He appeared to Dylan as the harbinger of everything evil. When Fix reached the curb, he stopped and slowly raised his hand as he beckoned Dylan to him.

"Watch my six and kick some ass," Dylan silently recalled.

The light inside Dylan's car ignited as he opened the door. He quickly closed it, checked his surroundings and stood motionless next to his car. He took his time and reexamined the entire field of combat. He sensed others were nearby. The scent of cologne and cigarettes were in the air, but their users were invisible in the murky darkness. Dylan inhaled, took a deep breath of fresh air and exhaled slowly. As he did, he released all of his unwanted nervousness as he confidently stepped into the fray.

"Where is Mary?" Dylan impatiently demanded of Fix. "She better be just fine, or I'm going to hurt you real bad."

Fix snapped his fingers and a man dressed in camouflage came out of Mary's door with her in tow. Once they were outside, the man shook her by the collar to speak. "I'm fine, Dylan," she calmly said. "The three of them haven't hurt me."

"Good, Mary, go back inside," Dylan replied. He was relieved to see that Mary wasn't hurt and that she informed him how many men he opposed. "Only three, Fixie? I knew you didn't have the balls to take me on yourself and now your entire crew knows it too." Dylan laughed at Fix and watched as two men attempted to outflank him.

Dylan had to control the flow of the fight. He moved backwards into the street and checked his surroundings to be aware of any objects that could be used as weapons. Once Dylan found his spot, he stopped and assumed his fighting stance as he prepared himself for the assassins.

The two hired fighters attacked Dylan from each side. Dylan faked left and threw a spinning rear jump kick that connected to the throat of the man on the right, who immediately grabbed his neck and gasped for air. He bent forward as he fought for breath when Dylan delivered a lightning fast snap kick to the side of his head, which knocked him out cold. His head thumped as it hit the street. Dylan spun quickly and located his remaining adversaries. He taunted them saying, "Come on, Fixie, haven't you got someone who can fight?"

Dylan's next opponent stepped up, squared off and in a deep voice said, "How about you try me on for size?" With that, Dylan's new adversary threw a series of fast kicks and punches. Dylan blocked them and returned with flying kicks and inside hand techniques. The two spun and flew at each other as if it were a part of a choreographed dance. Neither fighter was willing to give an inch as they showed the quality of their training and conditioning. After several rounds of back and forth sparring, they backed off and circled.

"Nice style. Too bad you're working for that jerk-weed Fix." Dylan said as a back-handed compliment.

The two combatants continued to circle and the gap between them slowly shrank. Dylan readied himself by gently closing his eyes as he connected with everything around him. He relaxed and followed the sound of a wisp of cool breeze as it swept past him, entered the trees and rustled their leaves. That was when he heard the assassin—he was about to strike.

Dylan dropped low and spun. But his move was anticipated and he was hit with a side kick that sent him to the ground. Dylan quickly pushed himself upward only to be struck in the temple with another kick that nearly knocked him out. He shook his head as he tried to clear his mind and get himself back onto his feet. But his opponent stepped over him and jammed his boot down hard on Dylan's back, pinning him face-down on the wet street. Without hesitation, the assassin pulled out his weapon, aimed squarely at Dylan's spine and fired. The blast echoed sharply off all the surrounding buildings. Dylan loudly moaned as intense pain raged through his back. A moment later, a second shot rang out from the assassin's gun. "No," said Dylan as he forcefully flipped himself over. "It's not going to end like this." He held his breath as sharp pain raged through his body. Blood began to run freely from his mouth as the assassin stepped over a helpless Dylan, pointed the gun at his heart and readied the finishing shot.

A misty rain started to fall and Dylan felt its cool wetness as it hit his face.

"Don't finish him yet," Fix commanded. "He's mine." Fix edged closer and enjoyed the feeling as he looked down at a defenseless Dylan. His mocking smile grew as he pulled out his own revolver and said, "It's time for you to die."

Dylan's entire body tensed as Fix took aim at his face. Fix wanted Dylan's eyes locked onto the bullet that would kill him. "Do me a favor, sweetie," Fix scoffed as he sadistically grinned. "Say hello to daddy for me."

A loud clap sounded as Mary's front door forcefully flew fully open and crashed into the side of the building. Fix looked up startled as she charged out of her house and onto the street. The assassin grabbed Fix's arm and quickly spirited him into the shadows. "The kid's finished. Wanton said you can't get caught. Let's go." Together they stealthily moved through the darkness and away from detection.

Mary ran from her house and covered Dylan's lifeless body with hers. She would not let another bullet hit him tonight. She gazed at his pained expression and listened as he let out a low pitiful groan. Her heart broke because she knew that there was nothing she could do. She began to cry as she gently stroked his hair.

Blood ran from Dylan's mouth as his eyes blinked open. He looked into the night sky and held his breath as he winced in pain.

"Hold on, Dylan. Friends are coming," Mary whispered.

Still sobbing, she sat up, looked to the heavens and let out a mournful wail that shattered the silence of the night. "Dylan's dead! Oh God! No! He's dead!" Her cry echoed through the trees and down the street.

The slimy smile of Mr. Fix grew even larger as he and his killer snuck back to their car unseen. They sank into the darkness, opened their car windows and quietly waited for the show to begin.

This homicide, like so many others, seemed to unfold like a three-act play. There was an opening act with a tearful realization, a quest for all the answers and an inevitable conclusion. The arrival of the police on the scene was the beginning of the murder investigation and also the start of Act 1.

Officers swarmed and secured the area while detectives questioned anyone and everyone to find answers. All the while, Mary tearfully sat on the curb with a lone officer as she verbally reconstructed her version of the night's events. She outlined everything she remembered as he silently sat with her and scribbled notes. Her emotions ran high.

As more squad cars and more officers arrived, Act 2 had begun. The flashing lights that overly illuminated the night sky woke the neighborhood from its sound slumber. All types of people slowly left the safety of their secure homes, milled around the scene and collected the gory details of what had recently transpired. How did this happen? How will this tragedy affect me?

When the coroner and all his people eventually arrived, Act 3 was well underway. The crime scene was scoured for additional evidence which was collected, inspected, bagged and categorized. It was obvious from all the activity that the coroner's department was determined to find the clues that would ultimately solve this murder.

Fix enthusiastically watched as Dylan's motionless body was placed into a bag and finally into the coroner's vehicle. Fix couldn't have been more pleased with himself.

Then, one by one, the deputies departed and the bright lights eventually disappeared. The neighborhood became quiet and its inhabitants soon forgot all that had transpired. Except for the two people who sat on the curb—Mary and the cop who was consoling her. She sobbed uncontrollably.

Fix smiled as he listened to her agony. After he felt that there was no more enjoyment to be had, he rolled up his window, took out his cell and placed a call. He was almost giddy as he said to Ezra, "One down, one to go."

"Are you damn sure?" Ezra demanded.

"I personally did the deed, I watched him take his last breath and I waited until the coroner put him in a bag. Dylan is dead," gloated Fix.

"Good."

# chapter 28

"JESUS CHRIST, RICK, DON'T touch that! That really hurts," Dylan whined as I poked at the two softball sized bruises on his back. "I didn't have time to ready myself for the first shot and damn, when it hit me, it hurt big time." Dylan winced and tried to reposition himself on Mary's couch as he recalled what it felt like to get shot. "Rick, next time, you're definitely going to be the catcher."

"Stop acting like such a girl, Dylan. Those bruises will be gone in a week... or so. Maybe a little more. But what's important was that we bought you the best bulletproof vest we could find, didn't we? What else could be done?" I paused and flashed one of my smiles. Secretively, I was ecstatic it wasn't me getting shot. "Good thing you went up against Gat. I know he protected you."

"Sure, I was glad too... Until he shot me! TWICE! IN THE BACK!!" he yelled for emphasis. But then he conceded, "Out there on the street... got to admit, Gat had some skills."

"Yeah, I guess that's one way to look at it, D. The way I heard it was that he kicked your ass." I laughed and Dylan flipped me off. "Seriously... what we really should be talkin' about is the fact that you almost did get shot in the face."

We both stopped and locked eyes as we soberly considered what had transpired. Too close, that entire thing was way too close. I kept on point and asked, "You going to be ready for tomorrow?"

Dylan winced again as he nodded, then he turned his attention to Mary, "So tell me, Mary, what took so damn long for you to come out of your house? That asshat Fix could have shot me... for real!"

Mary blinked her doe eyes and said, "You've got to remember that I was the one with all the responsibility here." She kept her eyes glued on his as she continued, "First thing first, I had to call Vinny to get him and all of his people out there right away. That was job number one, ya know. Then, while I had Vin on the line, we started gabbin' about some family stuff. You know... the things I was makin' for dinner on Saturday and the stuff he was bringin'. That's when it suddenly hit me...." Mary lightly tapped her forehead as she recalled, "I was supposta run outside and save your little butt." A look of shock crossed Dylan's face as Mary let out a hard laugh at him and finally confessed, "I'm kidding. Dylan, I had to wait for the right moment. Everybody in the theater business knows that timing is everything."

Mary beamed as she snapped her fingers and spun around. "Oh, oh and my encore... it was absolutely incredible." Her voice lowered an octave to overly dramatic tones as she recalled her closing scene. "After everyone had gone and the street was empty, the young beauty sat with the dashing police officer on the curb. Her tears flowed uncontrollably as she remembered her dear lost friend." Mary smiled to herself as she came out of her dream state and said, "My performance was Oscar caliber, absolutely Oscar-worthy... if I say so myself."

I stood and softly clapped for our Best Supporting Actress. We all agreed she was amazing in the role. As I sat down I made sure I had their attention and talked candidly. "That was the most difficult thing we've ever done. The truth is—it totally scared the hell out of me and I know it scared the hell out of both of you too." I took a sip on my coffee and thought for a minute before I said, "Today is Saturday. The bank gave us until Monday at 8am and we've still got a shitload of things to accomplish. It's going to be close." I changed the subject and asked, "How about we finish what we've started. We need to arrange a funeral."

"I'll drive," Mary stated. "And after we do our funeral home thing, I've planned to stay in character all day." She struck a movie star pose and repeatedly ran her fingers through her hair.

"Shotgun." I yelled even though it was just Mary and me.

The funeral home was owned by another distant relative of Mary, a guy named Jim Ripkin. We've all been friends with Jim's family for years and have been to graduation parties at his home for both of his kids. Oddly enough, when Jim parties, he always wears his black funeral suit.

"I've never done a deceitful thing in all my years of business," Jim said as he met us at the door with a grim look and handshake. As we moved through his lobby, he looked directly at me when he said, "It already happened, Rick.

As we found chairs in Jim's office, Mary said, "We really appreciate you helping us out, Jim. I know this whole thing is kinda weird. But believe me when I tell ya that this means a lot to us." She settled in and asked, "You were sayin' something already happened?"

"Exactly what Rick said would happen," Jim responded. "We received a call at the home this morning from a guy who asked about the services for Dylan Strong. So I told him that we haven't finished the arrangements but services would be held within the next couple days. Then the guy said that he wanted to send flowers and would like to dictate a note to me over the phone. So I wrote it down," Jim finished. "Take a look."

Heard you died.
Bummer.
Ezra

"I've had some pretty crazy condolence letters, but this one..." Jim said as he smiled and shook his head. "You boys musta pissed somebody off big time. Do you still think that he'll stop by and ask questions?"

"He might. He wants to make sure Dylan is dead. So we need you to make him believe the funeral services will happen just as you said." I looked at Jim and reiterated an earlier point, "This is important to us and we really appreciate all that you're doing."

"Hey, I'd do anything to help you guys out cuz of what you did for my kids." Jim stopped and looked at both of us.

"What did we do, Jim?" I asked.

He quickly realized that I had no idea what he was talking about.

"It was only a couple years ago when the economy was real bad and you guys gave both of my kids jobs. That was huge cuz when you did that, you also gave them a future. To me, it was the coolest thing ever since I know for a fact that your company wasn't hiring and hadn't hired a soul for months. You didn't have to do that... but you did it outta the goodness of your hearts. I'll always be grateful. So I say, whatever I can do for you in your hour of need... we're all good."

As we got in the car to leave I said to Mary, "I forgot his kids worked for us."

Mary gave me one of her looks and said, "Sometimes I wonder how you remember anything." Then she added one of those dismissive hand waves.

Once we returned to the office, our ruse continued. We fed Ezra exactly what he wanted to hear as Mary came in and sat down crying nonstop. "What are we going to do?" she asked through her light sobs. "Can we still be a company without Dylan?"

I followed her lead and said weakly, "I don't know, Mary. I can't think that far into it. I'm not sure what I should do," I paused. "Whatever we decide, we need to get rid of Ezra. I've considered the idea of just giving him what he wants. Maybe then he'll stop hurting everyone around me."

"You can't! Not after what he did to Dylan," she tearfully stated. She raised her voice as she declared, "We can still do this, Rick. The product is coming in and the bank is behind us. We can do this and we should 'cause we owe it to Dylan."

We both sat quietly and tried not to excessively overplay our parts. The silence was broken when my desk phone seemed to erupt. I turned down the volume as I checked Caller ID. It was Detective Vinny DeMano. He, along with his friends and associates, really stepped it up for us last night when we needed them the most.

Mary confided earlier that Vinny probably felt like he had to be there to help because it was a family payback thing. She told me that when he needed to prepare for the cyber division exam, she went to his apartment to study every day for over a month. He aced the exam. So after what she did for him, without a single complaint or thought of pay back, he felt it was his obligation to pay her back. She was family after all. Nothing you wouldn't do for family, right?

Vinny wanted to fill us in with the details of the police investigation into Dylan's shooting thus far. He also wanted to layout some disinformation for Ezra at the same time. For that reason, we put the call on speaker. "Hey, I'm glad I caught you, Rick. I thought we should discuss the forensic findings that surrounded Dylan's shooting. Is this a good time?"

"Sure, Vin," I said as down-hearted as I could. "What have you uncovered?"

"There were definitely three assailants. We arrested one guy at the scene. A local gun for hire with a long list of priors. We've had him in interrogation since last night but he still hasn't rolled on his buddies. Slow goin' tryin' to break him, but we got some help. The DA has stepped in and tried to speed this thing up. He approved the usage of our Advanced Interrogation Techniques Protocol. It's pretty scary stuff. It's like a Guantanamo detention center right here in the big city. Believe me when I tell ya, once they apply that level of pain, he'll definitely want to talk to us. Even if he doesn't, with the information we collected at the scene, our confidence level is very high that we will apprehended the other two soon. The net is closing in on them and it won't be long until we have 'em in custody."

I looked at Mary and restated what Vinny had said loudly enough for Ezra's listening benefit, "Let me get this straight, Vinny. You think the department is close to catching the hired assassins?"

"Yeah, I do." Vinny informed. "But that doesn't mean you're safe. Dylan was just the first to be targeted by this maniac. He wasn't the only name on the contract. Remember that and be sure to be careful."

"Thanks, Vinny. I'll be safe. I appreciate everything you've done. Do me a favor, when you are about to apprehend Dylan's killer, call me. I want to be there."

"Sure, Rick. You'll be there. Just don't do anything stupid."

I decided Ezra had enough 'news' and that he was ready for my call.

"What do you want? I'm busy," Ezra answered. "Oh, by the way, so sad about your idiot brother."

I sucked in air and held my tongue. I was the one who had to control the dialogue. "This has got to stop, Wanton," I firmly stated with a touch of remorse. "No one else needs to be hurt. Tell me exactly what you want."

"Want? Are you too thick to understand that yet? I want the damn company, I want the product and maybe I'll take more... what have you got left to offer?" I could hear him as he sucked deeply on his cigarette. He loudly exhaled as he said, "I want the ownership papers for the company signed and delivered to me. And, you're going to be the one delivering them."

"Fine, but I choose the location."

"Don't screw with me, Rick, and make sure you come alone. I wouldn't want to read about Mary or her son having an accident," Ezra condescendingly threatened. "Send me the details and make sure it happens tonight."

# chapter 29

I SENT EZRA DETAILS about where and when I wanted to meet. I decided that the vacated facility formerly used by the Rightway Can Company was ideal. It was large, empty and gave me tactical advantages. After the summer Dylan and I spent there, I completely knew the layout and was confident that I could navigate the interior of the building in the dark. This was the perfect place for me to permanently terminate our unwanted relationship. I told Ezra to be there at ten.

At nine forty-five I pulled up to the building and parked in the lot just a few paces from where Dylan and I had fought off the Hillbilly Nation. It had been over a decade since I'd seen the place and it was obvious that time hadn't been particularly kind to the building or the surrounding area. Every window was broken out, graffiti covered most of the walls and signs were posted by the city that declared the building unsafe. Tonight the place was desolate and darkness shrouded the entire area.

From where I parked, I could see that a single door-way had been pried open, one that led directly to my old department, tin plate. Ezra must have arrived early. I turned off the engine and took a minute to breathe in some fresh air. It smelled like winter was coming and the temperature was low enough that I could see my breath.

I reconsidered my mental check list for the tenth time as I looked down at my watch. It was time for me to go. I inhaled deeply and took the first step. A sense of trepidation washed over me as I walked toward the entrance into the old building.

As I edged past the opened door, I expected something or someone to be there. Gratefully there wasn't. I stopped and let my eyes adjust to their new surroundings. Cascading piles of trash lined the walls and the rats that were once only in the train shed were now clearly visible as they ran from my presence. The proud manufacturing facility was now overrun with filth and in complete disrepair. As I moved past the entrance into the building, the cloud-covered moonlight softly beamed through the broken windows and barely illuminated my old department. My skin crawled as I felt invisible adversaries watching. I slowed and peered as deeply as I could into the darkness.

The bare bones of the scavenged machines littered the department floor and were the only things immediately visible in the spotty moonlight. I peered deeper into the darkest edges of the large space and noticed the flickering of two small lanterns positioned on the floor near what was once the department's office. This was probably part of Ezra's poor attempt to set an evil mood. I walked slower now as I surveyed the entire area and expected trouble from any direction. As I drew nearer to the light, Ezra positioned himself directly in my path between the lanterns. Their light cast eerie flickering shadows on the floor and walls around him. I sensed he wasn't alone as he jeered at me.

"Nice to see you finally made it, Rick," he said as he wheezed and let out a congested cough. "Why did you ever choose such a rank place?" Ezra cleared his throat and spat on the floor. "Not at all a good way to start our partnership, Rick. Looks to me... like you don't trust me."

"Nostalgia, I guess."

"Well, that's just lovely Rick," dismissed Ezra. "Now that we've shared a moment and completed all the formalities, it's time to get down to business." Ezra took a small step toward me.

As he neared, I caught a wisp of his nasty scent. "Ezra, you really should shower and reconsider that stench you call cologne. You reek, big boy."

"Frankly, Rick, I don't give a shit what you think. I'm only in this God forsaken place because I want those signed contracts." Ezra now sounded more like himself as his tirade continued to grow. "It's time, Rick. Hand them over to me and stop screwing around." He held out his hand and wiggled his fingers as if he expected me to put the contracts in them.

Before I had a chance to respond to Ezra's demands, I was distracted by approaching footsteps that echoed wildly in the empty space. I leaned to my side and peered into the blackness as I waited for whomever to materialize. From the shadows behind Ezra the dark shape of Mr. Fix emerged and slowly became visible. I couldn't help but notice that he was holding his revolver and that it was pointed directly it at me. He took his time and casually drifted next to Ezra. He stood silently and taunted me with his cheap smile. I really disliked this guy.

"Have I got your attention now, Rick?" Ezra questioned with greater confidence. "Just give the papers to me and this will all be over," he said with all the conviction of a hangman.

I reached into my pocket and slowly brought my hand out empty. "Sorry, Ezra, I musta left them in my other coat. Or maybe the dog ate 'em. Could be they got lost in the shuffle," I wisecracked back because I knew Fix wouldn't shoot until they had the contracts in hand.

"Let me help him remember, boss," Fix grunted as he inched toward me. "I'll get this done fast." Fix trained his gun at the center of my chest. "Better yet, I could do him like I did his brother and we could just take the papers."

I stood in front of the two of them and tried to appear unfazed as I watched Fix move his finger over the trigger. I imagined that he had toyed with this possibility earlier.

"Last chance, Rick, or Mr. Fix gets his way," Ezra said.

Fix grinned as he raised his gun. "Come on, boss, let me finish this." He inched closer yet and aimed his weapon as he waited for permission.

With his finger on the trigger, Fix suddenly froze in place. "Wait... did you hear that?" He stood motionless, held his breath and listened intently to the empty darkness. He was sure he had heard something. Then, like the softest whisper in the dark of the night, it happened again—it was behind him. "Pssssst."

Fix spun toward the noise and raised his gun. As he did, he was instantly blindsided by a burning cigarette that flew at his face, careened off his cheek and burst into thousands of flying projectiles made of burning embers and flaming hot ash. They sparked and danced around his head as hot debris flew into his eyes and mouth. He fought back the remains and defensively held up his hands as he squinted into the blurred darkness to see anything or anyone. From out of the murkiness, a man grabbed the hand that held the gun. In one deft move, Fix's arm was twisted backwards and contorted into a painful arm and wrist lock. Fix couldn't possibly escape.

Barely able to stand upright with his arm practically dislocated and his wrist at its breaking point, Fix's eyes cleared. Shock and disbelief simultaneously crossed his face. "You're dead!" he yelled, as he spat ash and soot. "I saw them put you into a bag!"

Dylan lunged forward and drove Fix face down onto the concrete floor. Their combined weight landed painfully on Fix's shoulder and pinned it to the ground. Dylan yanked the gun free from his hand and instantly cracked him hard enough to knock him unconscious. Fix moaned as he sank into the filth.

Dylan stood over Fix and spun the gun like he was in an old movie. "Not so tough," he scoffed. He moved from behind Ezra to my right flank. We stood shoulder to shoulder and faced our adversary as twins once again.

"Ya know... it's like I keep tellin' ya, Ezzie," Dylan said, "You just can't find good help these days."

"D, do you believe this idiot?" I turned to face Ezra and slowly, in my smarmiest tone, said, "You really are stupid!"

Ezra's contempt for us boiled over. It was obvious that he couldn't contain the hatred he had for both of us any longer. His words failed him as he searched to find the perfect phrase to show how deeply his disdain for us had grown. "You can't... Do you think...." He finally spat at us and restarted, "Do you actually believe I wasn't ready for your simpleton bullshit? Theatrics don't fool anyone," he cursed as he become more and more irate. "Now, you... nothings—give me those God damned papers!"

I looked at Dylan and he at me. We shared the same questioning expression as we turned back and looked at Ezra. I started with the obvious comment to clear up our misunderstanding. "Maybe you should take a moment here, Ezra. You may not have noticed, but we have the gun."

Ezra held up his right hand as he stated, "With one snap of my fingers, Dylan dies."

Dylan looked at me, then at Ezra as he snidely responded, "Everyone wants to shoot me first. Why not shoot Rick first sometimes?"

"Enough! I've had enough of your childish bullshit!" Ezra said as he took off his hat and waved it over his head like some deranged ringmaster about to introduce a new attraction as he loudly yelled, "Light 'em up, boys!"

His words reverberated across the factory walls as red laser dots appeared on each of our jackets. The assassins Ezra hired had taken up positions somewhere in front of us. Dylan and I both watched as the two glowing red dots moved from our heads to our chests. We refocused our attention to the now grinning Ezra, who spouted, "Put the gun down and tell me what you've got to say for yourselves now, losers." Ezra gloated over our shocked expressions. "Cat got your tongues?"

"This changes nothing, Ezra," I defiantly said. "You won't get away with this. We have friends who know we came here."

"And the police know our location. They'll easily piece this together and prove you were involved." Dylan quickly added.

"You pathetic suckers, I'll have ten alibis for my whereabouts before they get to my door. I have nothing to worry about." Ezra grinned as he pointed a crooked finger at us and continued. "But the two of you…" He waited a couple seconds, eyed us both and concluded, "I'm afraid you're alone here boys, and there's no one who will come and save you this time." He sadistically giggled.

We watched as Ezra checked over each shoulder and surveyed the old workspace. His yellow smile became even broader now that he fully recognized that there was no one left who could testify against him. His confidence swelled and he seemed almost giddy as he proudly bragged, "The police are such fools. They couldn't catch the flu in this town. When I had Judge Fairman eliminated, the police couldn't find enough clues to open an investigation, much less convict me. And boys, when we're done here with our little… complication… I plan to burn this place to the ground along with all the incriminating evidence. Sorry, boys, but I've won and you've lost." Ezra lit a smoke and snickered to himself as he toyed with the concept. He looked down at an unconscious Fix as he added, "Unfortunately, he'll have to die here with the two of you. He's weak. I'll make it look like he shot both of you in self-defense before he died."

Dylan glanced my way. His fearful expression had disappeared. He looked back at Wanton and asked, "You sure you got all your facts right?" Dylan and I looked down at our jackets and used our hands to 'brush away' the red laser dots. Once they disappeared, we watched Ezra as Dylan chided, "I think somethin' musta gone wrong, Ezzie."

Ezra stood silently dumbfounded. What had just happened? He blinked wildly as the shock of the deception permeated his thoughts. We ate this up with a spoon. His reaction was priceless. Absolutely friggin' priceless.

In an instant, Ezra's true self resurfaced. His eyes raged and he literally growled at us in anger. He immediately went on a venomous attack, "You bastards won't get away with this. I'll have my attorneys crawling so far up your asses that they'll see tomorrow before they're finished."

Ezra's tirade towards us continued non-stop. The unconscionable toxic venom that erupted from him revealed how deeply he hated everything and everyone. The depth of his loathing grew in intensity until it exceeded Dylan's ability to accept or endure. That was the moment when I saw Dylan's thoughts had turned dark. He picked up the gun and defiantly stared at Ezra.

Ezra sneered back at Dylan and spouted, "You haven't got the balls to shoot me, punk."

Dylan's expression remained unchanged as he countered, "This is for Dad." He slowly raised his right arm and pointed the gun at Ezra's face. With one smooth even movement, he pulled back the gun's hammer. We all heard it click. Dylan's eyes narrowed as he coldly contemplated ending Ezra's miserable life.

I watched as he loosened and tightened his grip on the gun. At some point I started to believe that he'd actually go through with this and permanently end this pestilence.

I saw that he was blinded by hate. So before this went too far I lightly touched his arm and said, "Dylan, think for a second about all this and what it will do… to you."

The gun remained pointed directly at Ezra's face as Dylan reasoned with me. "I know exactly what you're going to say, Rick. This isn't part of the plan. I know what you expect from me and I know that we're supposed to turn this scum over to the police. But I don't care anymore. This trash was responsible for all of our problems. He's lied, cheated and colluded with Alice to steal our futures, he's gloated over what he did to our friend Jeff and he threatened Mary and her son. Then, for just a second, think about the colossal waste of time it would be to run this animal through a trial."

Dylan took a deep breath and momentarily considered everything he had just said. He knew that this single act of vengeance would change him forever. He considered what he should do and instantly decided that everyone would be far better off if Ezra were gone. Without moving the gun from Ezra's face, he coldly stated, "I'm going to fast-track the whole process and take care of this business right here and now."

I stepped closer until I stood chest-to-chest with Dylan. I looked into his eyes and saw what this decision was doing to him. At that moment, I felt what he felt. "D," I pleaded, "listen to me. I know what we should do." I was inches from him as I calmly spoke, "Dylan, I think you're right. But we should do this together."

An astonished Ezra couldn't believe what he had heard. He stood motionless and wide-eyed as I extended my left arm toward the gun. I placed the grip in my palm and slid my index finger above Dylan's on the trigger. We held our arms outstretched and together as we pointed the gun at our enemy. All around us became eerily quiet. The only sounds were from the two of us as we inhaled and exhaled the cool night air—our breathing was in sync.

"Say something stupid," urged Dylan under his breath.

"You both aren't worth my spit. You're losers. And the lowest of you all was your stupid old man."

Once Ezra uttered those nasty words, Dylan and I simultaneously squeezed the trigger. A deafening blast sounded from the gun that shattered the silence of the night and reverberated loudly off the stone walls of the old factory. A look of total shock and surprise crossed Ezra's face as the bullet harmlessly whizzed passed his ear.

"Damn it, Dylan. You couldn't hit a barn if you were in it. You suck."

"Get real, Rick. You pulled the gun to the side and missed. Not me."

"I've always been a better shot than you. Admit it."

"I won the medals; I won best in school, not you, Rick."

"You're delusional, Dylan. What we need right now is an expert opinion."

"Fine, Rick." Dylan laughed to himself. "Go find yourself an expert opinion."

I stepped back, megaphoned my hands and loudly bellowed, "Yo, who missed that shot?" The sound of my voice echoed repeatedly off the walls.

As the last generation of my question faded away, a single voice spoke clearly from out of the darkness. "It was hard to tell from my vantage point, but I do believe it was Dylan who missed," confessed Detective Vinny DeMano as he appeared out of nowhere followed by a swarm of Chicago's finest. He laughed as he said, "I guess Dylan's aim was off due to all that playin' dead he did last night. Musta messed you up."

"This isn't happening! This can't be happening!" squealed a shocked non-believing Ezra as the police swarmed around him. "These two imbeciles aren't smart enough to pull off something like this."

"They are tonight," said Vinny as he slapped the cuffs on Ezra. "And by the way, thanks for your admission of guilt for the murder of the Judge Fairman. You are so finished, tough guy."

Instantly, Ezra realized what he had said and that he had incriminated himself. The uniformed officers escorted him from the building into a waiting squad cars.

All at once, the realization of what happened washed over me. Our ordeal had finally ended. I felt the weight of Ezra lift off our backs and, in its place, a sensation of overwhelming relief. We had won. Our plan worked and we actually won! When I checked out Dylan, his patented smile seemed noticeably broader.

"Lookin' good, D."

"Tell me somethin' I don't know, Rick."

# chapter **30**

**two weeks later**

A SINGLE CHAMPAGNE GLASS clinked over the commotion of the crowded hall. Thomas Rubin stood on his chair and rapped his glass with his shrimp fork as he asked for everyone's silence. Eventually, the room was still and all eyes focused on Thomas.

"Ladies and gentlemen," Thomas began. "My name is Thomas Rubin and I've been awarded the title 'Greatest Attorney in The Universe' by our hosts. Instead of being shy about this well-deserved title, I've decided to simply live with its burden. But I digress... I'm here tonight to let you all know that after an extensive police search of his home and office, evidence was found that contained details of every filthy crime Ezra Wanton and Mr. Fix ever committed. And, I'm glad to professionally report, they will undoubtedly spend the rest of their lives as guests of the state in the grey bar hotel." A loud cheer erupted from everyone in the room.

Thomas continued, "But, we are all here tonight for another, more important reason. So without further ado, I give you Rick and Dylan Strong."

Everyone in the room jumped to their feet and applauded. I was flabbergasted. Dylan and I put on this gala for all of them as our way to thank everyone who had been there for us when we needed them most. We wanted everyone to know how much we appreciated them.

There were so many friends and family here who joined in the celebration. They all beamed with smiles that glowed as bright as the morning sun. I was totally humbled. Dylan and I waded through the crowd and soaked up the good vibes as we went to Thomas. "Thank you Thomas," I said as I pulled him close. "Thank you for everything."

"It was my pleasure," replied our youngest brother.

I looked around at everyone who was there. In the center of the festivities, I saw Detective Vinny DeMano and the entire cyber unit including the coroner. They brought several baskets full of fresh-baked blueberry muffins to the festivities. The coroner laughed to himself when he told Dylan that his acting sucked and that he shouldn't give up his day job. Dylan told him that he was jealous.

The ever charismatic Gatlin Brown and some members of his inner circle were there. Once again, when we needed him the most, he saved us. Gat reached out and held us both. He told us that we would always be part of his family. We were honored.

I stepped back and scanned the crowded room, I saw so many faces who were instrumental in our success. Bob Rend and his team from the bank were there, all full of good wishes and handshakes. Jim Ripkin and his family were there. Both of his girls ran up and gave us hugs. Even Beau Reese, Dad's old attorney, gave a thumbs up and said that Dad would have been proud. Eveyone's excitement was contagious.

To top off the evening, our best friend, Jeff Kim, arrived. He was still recovering in a wheelchair and was casted, but he got on the dance floor and rolled out a few. After all he had endured, Jeff beamed as he introduced us to the new love of his life, his personal nurse, Apple Betty. She still hates the name.

"Thank you everyone," I said loudly into the mic to get their attention. "Dylan and I thank you from the bottom of our hearts. This celebration is for all of us. We stood as one and stopped really bad people from doing massive harm. We will always be in your debt."

Dylan wasted no time as he grabbed the mic out of my hand, pushed it high over his head and let out a primal scream that loudly echoed around the room. His screams were legendary and the crowd knew it was coming because the moment he stopped, the entire room screamed back.

Dylan looked out at the rowdy group and acted surprised. Then he flashed one of his patented smiles and yelled, "Let's PARRR-TAAYY!!"

The band blasted out its raucous beat and everyone spontaneously jumped onto the dance floor. The celebration was officially into overdrive. Everywhere I looked I saw friends who were happy. Their laughter grew and joy blossomed on every face.

Dylan was captivated by his new love, Lily West. He spun her around and around and around again as they danced. Lily giggled at Dylan and her eyes lit up as she fell into his arms for a long kiss.

I reached out my hand to Mary—she took it and squeezed it just a little. She looked so beautiful. Her gentle smile and her kind eyes warmed my heart. I wanted this moment to last forever. I gave Mary another warm hug and smiled to myself because that was when I realized that true happiness was in my life once again.